CR-76

MW01135766

Plum Duff

and other short stories

Carol Ann Ross

Copyright 2015 IRONHEAD PRESS

All rights reserved. No part of this publication may be reproduced in any form without permission of the author.

Cover design by C A Ross, S L Bruce

The short stories in this book are works of fiction. Names, characters and incidents are a product of the author's imagination and are used fictionally. Any resemblance to actual events or persons living or dead, is entirely coincidental.

Barnacle Bill's is a poem written by Dee Dee Paliotti Lloyd with her express permission.

The essay written by Diane Batts Geary is her work alone.

Other Books by Carol Ann Ross

THE DAYS OF HAIRAWN MUHLY
THE TRILL OF THE RED-WING BLACKBIRD
THE BRIDGE TO PARADISE
WATERLOGGED

TABLE OF CONTENTS

Acknowledgements

Thank you to the many people who helped me gather information—Chloe Blum, Caitlin Blum, Doug Thomas, James Brown and Randy Batts.

You have all been fountains of knowledge.

To Deb McKnight, Patti Blacknight, Bruce Blacknight, Shari Bruce, Gigi Oberlin, Lou Wilson and Cindy Ramsey. I would like to offer thanks for your technical support.

Dedication

This book is dedicated to two women whom I have known my entire life. Each is different than the other in many ways but the thing that bonds them, makes them similar in even more ways, is their love for the island.

Diane Batts Geary and Dee Dee Paliotti Lloyd are as much a part of Topsail Island as the scrub oaks and towers. My love and gratitude to you both.

FOREWORD

Writing a compilation of short stories is like putting on a new outfit—jeans and a tee shirt, a dress for church, a frilly blouse for an evening out and even old cut-offs and a worn pullover for ultimate relaxation. Each story is a different facet of the writer.

Short stories can be exploratory, insightful, or confusing. I found writing these to be fun.

I always marvel at where my poor old brain will take me—the old roads and new highways.

I hope you, the reader, will find as much enjoyment reading these as I did in writing them.

The Blue Run

A fishing story

Ira Hopkin quit school when he was fourteen years old. But in 1940 that was not an uncommon practice for the youth of fishing and farming communities in the southeast coastal areas of North Carolina.

Then, males that age knew most of what was needed to be proficient in their families' trades.

In that day and time, boys in rural communities were self-disciplined, hard working contributors to their families' well-being–generally speaking.

This was doubly true for Ira. Nothing derogatory could be said about young Hopkin's work ethic, that's for sure. Of the seven Hopkin children, Ira–the middle child–was probably the most diligent at the tasks he was asked to perform by either of his parents.

Albeit, being the only boy among six girls, the mores of the day allowed him little in the way of competition.

Even before quitting school, Ira was up at dawn with his father to begin the chores. And then, after the school bus deposited him at the top of the long

11

winding dirt path to his home, Ira scurried to either join his father in the fields or down by the sound where the skiff and dory were moored and where Henry Hopkin often sat designing fishing nets and seines for himself and other local fishermen.

Already Ira had learned that craft from his father and even at his young years considered himself a master seine maker. Henry did not argue the fact.

"The boy is a quick learner," the elder Hopkin often remarked.

After having learned to read, write and cipher, Ira had lost interest in school. The last couple of years he found it tedious and boring, though the teacher's monthly report indicated he was passing all subjects with flying colors.

Still, Ira carried a yearning to leave school. He would rather have been fishing in the ocean, flounder gigging in the sound or shrimping in sloughs. But he dare not mention this to his parents. He knew his good grades and the promise of a high school diploma was a source of pride to them.

He'd watched his father nod his head as he perused the grade card from school.

The gleam in his mother's eye was undeniable too, as Mae stood alongside her husband reading the comments from the teacher: everything was above average, everything indicated that Ira had the potential to be special.

Like so many, the Hopkins believed education was the only way to become successful and therefore a better person.

But Ira knew too that his father found joy spending the long days on the water with him.

It was different there—on the ocean where the sense of accomplishment was more powerful—much more powerful than the grade card from school.

There, on the water, the two shared a feeling of determination as they pulled on the net, or reeled in a big mackerel. They toiled together, sharing sweat and groans of exertion, then laughter when a task was completed.

It took both of them to do the task and once the fish were in the boat, there was the satisfaction of knowing there would be enough money to purchase things needed—even a few things wanted.

But the greatest sense of fulfillment came from the fishing experience itself—being part of the ocean; a feeling of the presence of the surrounding power—it was God-like. Nothing could compare.

Henry knew that salt water ran in his son's veins, as it did his. The farming, working the land and growing food was just a means to an end. He suspected his son felt that way too.

But like he always did, Ira and his father made sure the farming chores were completed—that the corn, beans and squash were planted and harvested. Those were the foods that got them through the winter.

Sometimes his sisters helped pick the crops, but normally it was just Ira.

There was the unspoken bond between them, the men, providing—using their brute strength, enduring the weather, nurturing their crops, sweating in the sun—while the women nurtured them and provided in their own ways—for the family.

And they were a family, each helping to make life as good as possible—each with their own foibles and personalities—different, but one.

But things were changing in the Hopkin household. Subtly at first—Ira suspected that the girls really didn't notice—but his mother did. He saw it in her eyes, her expressions.

14

Henry Hopkin just didn't seem to have the stamina he once did. He tired more easily and ate less.

Ira had noticed the bagginess of his father's trousers and the diminishing strength in his arms.

Because of his father's declining health, by the spring of 1939 Ira was doing most of the planting. It had to be done, but then as soon as he could, he readied the dory for fishing. Fishing was the best, according to Ira. He and his father agreed on that. Even Mae commented on the light in her "boys" eyes when they readied for a fishing trip.

"You always get your strength back when you know you're going fishing," she had commented on more than one occasion. And when spring rolled around Mae watched them repair any faults with the boats and busy themselves with mending any tears in the net.

With the spring came the running of the blue fish. They would be heading north from Florida, following pop-eye mullet and menhaden, as those smaller fish migrated north too.

Ira could not remember a time when he did not help his father with fishing in some way. The two went together, his father and the ocean. He could not imagine one without the other.

Both represented a world different than the one in the house they lived in. Was it because there, on the ocean, it was a man's world? He wasn't sure. But Ira knew he loved being on the water–that world where he breathed a different air.

Oh, his mother and the girls would help salt the fish and pack them in barrels to be sold to the markets. But they couldn't know or understand what it was like to be on the ocean.

His six sisters were like other young girls of their time, they did the cleaning and cooking, mending and tending. They stayed home or near it, and rarely ventured to the docks and were *never* on the water.

The two oldest had found beaus and married. Lilly now lived in Fayetteville with her husband Ralph and Clara had gone to Richlands with her husband Harold.

Eighteen year old Olivia, teased often for being boyfriend-less, was valedictorian of her class at Topsail School in nearby Hampstead and had applied for scholarships to attend the college in Wilmington. After graduation she would be moving there to live with Aunt Inez.

Soon, Ira would be the oldest of the Hopkin children at home. The thought warmed him, as he'd never liked being teased and bossed about by the older girls who always referred to him as baby brother. Perhaps that was why he'd always chosen to do things outside, particularly in one of the boats–far away from the girl's chiding. There he could be alone, be his own man, his own person. There, his sisters held no knowledge or interest.

Ira liked his older sisters. Yes, he even loved them, but for whatever reason, he knew he would not miss them terribly.

On the other hand, his younger sisters looked up to him, one or more was always asking for him to ride them on his shoulders or to push them in the tire swing in the yard.

Vera and Theda, were eleven and nine, respectively. They were starting to get a little big for him to carry around, but he did it nevertheless just to hear them giggle and brag about their big strong brother.

Little Gale, only five, and light as a feather, was the apple of his eye. She was referred to as the shy one. She rarely joined in the banter between him and the other sisters, rarely played with her doll and seemed to prefer digging in the soft spongy marsh where the hermit crabs lived.

The hem of her dress was muddy so often that Mae Hopkin eventually let her wear only her underpants outside to play.

Of course, she was teased by the other sisters and as a result, Gale kept her distance.

Suspecting that some of that shyness was feigned due to fear of ridicule, Ira felt a kindred spirit with the child.

Often when either was being teased by a sibling, the two would share-a knowing look. It was like they shared a secret—an unspoken one— somewhat like the bond he had with his father.

On days when Ira and Henry took to the water, Gale was the only one who would follow them down to the dock and watch as they motored the skiff around the stand of scrub oaks and out of sight.

Every once in a while Henry Hopkin would gather his daughter to pull her into the skiff and take her for a ride.

Ira usually steered while Gale sat on her father's lap. Above the roar of the outboard, Ira could hear very little that his father and sister said. But he did observe the tenderness of little Gale's hand reaching back to caress her father's face as he spoke softly into her ear.

If the catch had been poor or weather had driven them in early from the ocean, Henry would take his daughter out to fish for spots in the sound.

But they did not venture out through the inlet with Gale though she begged and begged.

Mae was adamant about not taking such a young child into the ocean. And Henry abided by his wife's wishes.

Still, in the evenings when Henry and Ira returned from a long day of working on the water, Gale would be waiting, waving as the outboard sputtered and as the boat was guided to its mooring.

She was the only sister to watch as father and son unloaded crates of seafood. She watched as Ira stood before the dockside table cleaning the fish, deftly settling the long thin knife beneath the pectoral fin before slicing the head off, then piercing the flesh just before the pelvic fin and dragging the knife back to let the guts spill out.

As he had learned from Henry, Ira described each organ and explained their use in the body of the fish before sweeping the innards away into the water.

"Is that right, Daddy?" Gale always turned to ask her father if Ira was correct in his descriptions.

Henry would nod as he stood silently next to his son, allowing the relationship between the two siblings to grow.

Gale was mesmerized by it all.

It was at her age that Ira had begun going out with his father to gather shellfish in the sound and troll for blues in the Atlantic.

Realizing how young a five year old really was, Ira was astounded that his father had let him go out beyond the inlet.

)()()()()()(

As Ira watched the dynamic of his family–their struggles as Henry Hopkin became less able to work outside in the fields or to ready the boats for fishing–the desire to leave school grew inside of him. Ira knew he could make things better if he could only work full time with his father.

Often he wanted to blurt out,–*Oh, how much better things could be if I left school and could help the family.* Ira thought this often. But he never said anything aloud.

Scenarios danced in his head as he yearned to contribute to the family well-being. Then he would be free on the ocean to catch mullet and blues or to gig flounder and gather shellfish in the sound. It made a lot more sense than sitting at a desk in a stuffy school house.

Then his father would not feel so burdened by not being able to provide for his family as he once had.

And though the elder Hopkin had never mentioned this—never spoken those words—Ira knew that it must have been the way his father felt. He read it in his eyes, in his slouched appearance.

As the weeks went by, his father's pain was undeniable. It was evident that Henry was getting worse. The hurt in his father's eyes was palpable.

They had always communicated silently—the wonder of being on the sea—the appreciation for the yield—being part of it all. What could be more grand? But now what emanated from the older man's eyes was the loss of those things. And Ira noticed as they rocked in the boat among the swells, the frequency of his father's gazing toward the horizon.

The acknowledgment of his father's diminishing abilities ached Ira's being.

One night as he watched his father move the bits of food around on his dinner plate, Ira blurted out, "I am not going to finish school and I do not want to go to college."

More words fell non-stop from his mouth. "I hate school, it's boring. I've learned all I need to learn. Please let me quit and help out more."

Both Henry and Mae shook their heads. It was an impossible suggestion. "You must finish school," they said in unison.

But each day Ira proclaimed his desire. Each day he added reasons and more reasons. He listed names of people he knew who were successful without a diploma and added, "I can't stand the teacher, I'm not learning anything, the kids are so childish," as another cause to quit.

The list of grievances grew as the days multiplied. Finally after enough weeks of complaining, his parents reluctantly consented to his dropping out.

Dreams of a college educated boy in the family flitted away like wispy clouds on a hot summer evening.

His mother cried. His father, worn and debilitated by effects of the disease that had slowly been ravaging his body, was not as hard to convince. He flashed a perceptive look, and then bowed his head.

Henry had been depending more and more on the boy for the last several months yet, hoping his increasing infirmities would not deter his son from bettering himself. But in the end, it seemed they had after all.

Henry Hopkin doubted he was much longer for this world and he knew the family needed food on the table and money to live.

He knew that more than likely he would be selling at least five of the seven acres of land his family lived on to pay the bills that had been accruing. And seeing how Ira loved the sea so much, he figured that was where the boy would choose his livelihood—the land could be sold, the ocean never would be.

Already he was talking with a few of the local folk about the purchase of his land. He knew there would be a buyer.

Having not told even his wife about the impending sales, Henry concentrated on teaching his young son the surreptitious behaviors of sea life, of the tricks of the trade—things he was sure he'd already instilled in the boy—but things he felt determined to reinforce. It brought him both joy and sorrow as he observed how much a part of it all his son already was.

He saw it in the sweat of Ira's brow and the deep breaths his son took on humid days after a heavy rain, breathing in the salt and expanse before him—in the exhaustion the two experienced after hauling in a catch, wet with the sea, sweat and heavy salt air.

)( )( )( )( )(

Nearly a year had passed and Henry was no longer able to join his son in oyster gathering. The previous four months of the shellfish season, he had found himself growing weaker and weaker and now the season was nearing a close. He had hoped he would be able to at least make it until April when the blue fish ran. They filled the water, roiling with their angry activity as they chased smaller fish.

He had always loved going out in the dory with his son and either trolling or using the net to catch the blues. His favorite was trolling, the yield was perhaps not as robust as with a net, but so much more exciting.

The thrill of the fight—Henry always loved a good fight and was never one to give up easily. Blue fish always gave a good fight.

Resting in the overstuffed lounger, Henry pictured tying the lures with monofilament, attaching a header with a flat silver spoon, then setting the poles in their slots. Those on the transom he let out about seventy-five feet. The angled poles at either side of the boat, he let out about one hundred feet.

As he thought, his eyes gathered in deep wrinkles at the corners, the corners of his lips curled upward. He felt the rock and sway of the little nineteen foot dory beneath his feet; his mind wandered. It was a sunny day with a mild cooling breeze

His mind wandered once again–and then there was his daughter's graduation–Olivia was the first of the Hopkin family to graduate from high school and the first to attend college.

Henry's heart swelled with pride as he closed his eyes and felt the breeze off the sea sweep through his thick graying hair. A smile settled on his lips as his last breath escaped them.

"The blue run in the spring and fall." Ira stepped down into the dory from the narrow wooden dock, then smiled up to his sister, Gale.

"But why? How do they run?" A puzzled looked crossed her brow.

"They swim, okay? They swim, we call it run." Ira scrunched his nose and jerked gently on one of his sister's braids.

"Where are they swimming?" she asked.

"This time of year, in the fall, they are heading back to Florida. Back where it is warm."

"Oh." The little girl bit her bottom lip, narrowed her eyes and spoke. "I want to go too." She twisted her brown pigtail and picked at the rubber band at the end of the strand.

"To Florida?" Ira teased.

"No, with you."

"Ha, the fish would pull you in—they're near about as big as you."

Squinting her eyes against the morning sun, Gale pursed her lips. "Daddy takes me with him sometimes."

Cocking his head to the side, Ira studied his sister's face. The innocence there was overwhelming. Her innocence and curiosity had always tugged at his heart strings.

"Daddy *used* to take you," he corrected. "And Daddy's not here now. Besides, I'm going out in the ocean. Daddy only took you in the sound, never the ocean."

Gale's eyes dropped to search her feet. "He's in heaven." The girl caught her brother's eyes and drew her lips into a line, "Daddy would take me with him. I'm older now. I'm in school now. If Daddy was here now, I know he'd take me—s'not fair."

"S'not?" her brother snickered and winked, "snot?" He mimicked her again then wiped a make believe bugger from his nose.

"Ewww!" Gale curled her lips, then giggled loudly.

There was no doubt that his little sister had her father's smile. Ira lingered a bit as he watched her laugh. "I'll bring you back a big ol' blue." He called loudly.

"Well, hop to it, then." Gale placed her hands on her hips, the smile and laughter having disappeared.

She sure does look like Dad. Ira caught himself staring at her again.

"Brother?" the little girl questioned.

Ira shook his head and laughed. "Go on back to the house now. I know Momma's wondering where you're at."

Gale turned around and around, twirling her homemade dress. "Bring me back a sea shell–a big one!" She ran toward the tire swing near her home.

Turning his attention toward the sound, Ira pulled sharply on the pull start cord and moved the tiller of the outboard to propel him toward the open water.

The laughter left his eyes immediately as he faced the breeze blowing in from the north. He could feel the familiar emptiness. It had been with him since his father's passing.

He'd missed the spring run so this would be the first time he'd ever been fishing for blues without his father. He knew he would miss the man even more as he went through the inlet into the Atlantic.

If Henry had been with him, they would have thrown the net–used that to catch the blues. Two men were needed for the net.

He glanced at the long poles lying on the deck.

A gull passed overhead. Squawking loudly, it circled again.

Was that the old man telling him to ready the rods, to set the lures—or was it just another noisy bird flapping its wings in the wind?

Before, when he and his father had trolled, they had split the poles, each working two. It was fun, especially when they were trolling right through the middle of a school.

Wham, wham, wham, wham. One after the other struck the lines. Then, whir, whir of the reels as they wound the mono back onto it. Sometimes he could feel the heat from the reel as it wound so tightly and fast.

A smile curled his lips for a second as he turned the boat into the choppy inlet.

Today was not too bad. Motoring through the inlet rolled the boat around a bit, but that was normal. There was always a bit of tease to the inlet.

Reaching beyond the last wave, Ira looked to the right, starboard, where Henry had always perched along the gunwale. He gulped emptiness as he moved out beyond the breakers. There were no swells on the horizon—it would be a calm day.

What did he expect today? He'd brought six crates for fish. He hoped to fill them all.

Most of the catch would be salted down and taken to market. He'd keep a few for dinner, though he'd never really liked eating blues. To Ira they were too bloody a fish, too strong. He preferred mullet, grouper or snapper.

He shrugged his shoulders, "Maybe I'll get lucky today and catch a couple of those."

As the dory glided past Lea Island, Ira waved to the few fisherman on the shore casting their lines. They waved back as he passed. Turning the tiller, Ira headed south and farther out.

He figured a half mile would do just fine and he slowly guided the craft through the still water. Barely a ripple stood on the glass like surface; it twinkled various hues of gray and silver, green and blue. Turning the motor off, he heard the slapping of the water against the hull.

In a moment it would stop as the wake from the dory settled into the vast expanse.

Gazing at the poles once again, Ira stared for a moment before realizing the time had slipped by with nothing to show for it.

"Hop to it, boy," he said aloud, recalling his sister's words from earlier. Those were the words his father had used on occasion when he had found him daydreaming. The image of Gale's face and the hands on hips stance she had posed earlier, came to mind again.

He had throttled down to a slow one or two knots and baited the poles, set them in the holders and watched as he let the lines out—he followed their lines as they cut into the water.

Stepping back to study the poles, watching the thin trace of line through the still ocean waters, he positioned himself in front of the outboard and adjusted the throttle to increase the speed a few knots more.

The boat cut a gentle path through the water, allowing the lines to follow behind.

Ira leaned back against the gunwale and relaxed into looking at the colors and swaths of clouds above him. The placid slap, slap of the ocean lulled him into a drowsy consciousness.

"Boy!" It was his father's voice. Ira lifted his face to meet the man's eyes. Their steely gaze focused on one pole. It bent as the line whirred. Ira jumped to his feet and pulled the pole from the holder. Quickly he wound in the line. Just then two more of the poles bowed. And just as the fourth pole arched, Ira reached to push the throttle down, slowing the boat.

He reeled in the lines as quickly as he could, released the hooks from each fish's mouth and reset the lines.

Pushing the throttle back to a slow troll he perched himself once more against the gunwale, but this time he sat alert—prepared now for more strikes—more blues.

And they came, one right after the other. Sometimes all at once. There was no stopping for respite, just continuous unhooking, re-baiting, and the thunk, thunk of slamming the poles back into their holders.

Between breaths, it seemed, he threw fish into the crate boxes. He searched for a rhythm to move through the work but was unused to working alone and many fish fell to the deck. He was aware that many of the catch had been lost, simply because he could not get to a pole in time. Oh, how he wished his father was there to help.

Before, with his father, he'd always had time to think about things. To work into a rhythm with his father—reel, unhook, throw, re-bait. Reel, unhook, throw, re-bait. There was time then. There were two then.

Now he had no time for rhythm—or time to build one—and certainly very little time to avoid the sharp teeth of the blues. They were notorious for gouging fingers and wrists.

In the midst of all the rushing, while setting a line, he did notice blood running down his arm toward the elbow. But there was no time for tending to that, the line needed set, the spoon pulled from the fish's mouth. And it would be repeated again and again.

Oh how he wished he had someone to help him, someone who knew how to work a net. He ached for his father.

Then it was still again, all at once. No strikes, no hurrying to toss fish into boxes. He took this time to move the crates around and pick up fish still flopping in the bottom of the boat. He breathed a sigh as he tossed the last one in a box.

The sea was still calm. Usually after noon, a breeze would kick up and there would be a little more swell to the water, but not today.

Ira drew his lips in tight and searched the horizon, letting his eyes wander to the land only a few hundred yards away.

Land was a different world—he had given up trying to explain the difference between being on the ocean and being on land. But he knew there was one. Sighing heavily, he continued to study the coastline.

Shortly he noticed a few fisherman on the beach. He could barely hear the laughter and squeals from the children running along the shore near them. It looked like they were with their families and were having a picnic.

He and his family had done that at times. It was always fun. His mother and sisters gathered driftwood for a fire and he and his dad caught fish.

The girls played in waves and dug holes to make sandcastles.

He and his father cleaned the fish and then his mother and the older of the children helped cook them up.

When the fish were ready to eat, the family would sit on a blanket from home and enjoy the day's catch along with some corn bread and cole slaw his mother had packed in a basket.

Ira recalled those times with fondness as he waved back to the people on shore.

Moving back to his spot against the gunwale, Ira drowsed once again. He pushed on the throttle to move the boat ahead. It purred gently as the boat glided gradually northward.

How long was it before again in some hazy dream Ira heard the words "Well done." The sarcastic tone was undeniable.

Once again the whir of lines filled the air, jolting the youth to his feet. Slipping on the now slimy sole of the boat, Ira caught his balance as he grabbed the gunwale and pulled himself erect. Instantly he scolded himself for not rinsing down the deck with sea water. Well done?

How many times had Henry chided him for forgetting something important? Ira belted a laugh, loud and raucous. "Okay, Daddy. I hear you."

Enthusiastically Ira grabbed a pole, reeled it in, whipped the spoon from the blue's mouth and cast the fish into a box.

He let the line out , stepped to another pole, reeled, tore the spoon from the fish's mouth and cast it into a box. Again and again, he moved methodically about the poles—his legs balancing the rock of the boat with the movement of the ocean as if they were one. He reeled in another line, took the fish, threw it in the box—he had found the rhythm.

Pleased with himself as he worked, he found even more pleasure when he found on the end of a line a grouper. Just as quickly and without missing a beat, he threw the fish into a bucket near the bow of the boat.

There was no time to even think about time and before he knew it two more crate boxes were filled to overflowing.

The sun sat hazily on the western sky. A chop had developed and the poles stood still, lines all reeled in, with no bend or sound except the clickety-click of the spoon hitting the pole intermittently. Ira licked his lips. They were salty. Once again he rested against the gunwale. He breathed a deep sigh of contentment. It had been a good day.

He reached into a cooler, pulled out a bottle of Pepsi Cola and popped the cap against the gunwale. He studied the marks from previous bottle openings of he and his father and exhaled a long breath.

The cola tingled his throat as he tilted his head back to drink its contents. Tossing the bottle overboard, Ira watched it fill with water and sink.

The haze of the day belied the depth and though he could have sworn he was in a good twenty feet , Ira could see the sandy bottom below. A few small fish darted about. He watched a bigger one fast behind it.

"Always a bigger fish out there somewhere."
He laughed to himself.

Still studying the water, he spotted a whelk. It was a fine whelk, somewhat pink with strands of blue running through it. He thought of Gale's request.

Should I? he thought. Grabbing the lip of the gunwale Ira pulled himself up and over and into the cool October water.

He was not prepared for the chill that swallowed his body but he ignored it as he swam down and down toward the shell.

How far can this be? he wondered. Now, it seemed so far away. Still he persisted in reaching the shell with his arms stretched and straining to touch it. He could feel the cold. It was not biting cold, but he was starting to feel it in his bones, in his groin.

Finally his outstretched finger wrapped around the whelk. He closed his eyes for a moment; he caught a scent, perhaps it ran through his mind. But the scent was there nonetheless, It was his father's. Ira swept his body to turn and move upward toward the light.

)()()()()(

As he pulled the boat around the stand of oaks, the wooden dock came into view. Sure enough, Gale sat swinging her legs from the side, her bare toes toyed with the shadowy water below.

Already her face beamed a smile; leaning back on her elbows she laughed loud and hard. "I knew it, I knew it!" she shouted. "I knew you'd come back with lots and lots of fish."

"How do you know I've got lots and lots of fish, miss smarty pants?" Ira called as he pulled the boat closer to the dock.

"I can smell 'em, brother."

"Well, can you smell this?" He tossed the whelk near to where Gale stood.

Picking it up, she poked at the white meat still inside. "Momma cooks this really good—makes real good fritters with it."

Ira nodded. "Sure does."

"It's really pretty, Ira. Thank you for the shell, it'll be so pretty on my window sill."

Ira nodded again as he began stacking the boxes of blue fish onto the dock.

Gale watched as he pushed one box next to the other. She noticed the long line of blood along his arm.

Studying his fingers she saw too where the skin was torn and had left dried blood stains.

She touched a finger to the bloodied arm and then to her lips, "It's salty–it runs in your veins doesn't it?"

Ira casually looked at his blood stained hands and arms, "Ha! Those blue devils will tear a hunk out of you, if they can. They don't want to die either."

"That's what Daddy always said. That salt water ran in your blood just like his." The girl pulled a crate box close to the cleaning table on the dock and reached in to grab a blue. Placing the thin blade beneath the pectoral fin, Gale pulled the knife hard against the body of the fish, the head separated neatly and she pushed it into the water below then slid the blade along the pelvic fin. "I've got salt water in my veins too."

TUPPER

A little dog story

Marla tilted her chin upward and stretched her neck as she studied the darkening clouds overhead. She looked toward Jerry, standing several feet away, his attention focused on the progression of high school bands and clowns parading down Front Street.

His back turned slightly away from her, Marla noted Jerry's unkempt hair and attire–he didn't look nearly as attractive as he had the first time she'd met him.

Lately, he seemed somewhat annoyed with her; he even refused to meet her eyes since this morning when she picked him up and the other two friends, Bell and Pete, to attend the Azalea Festival in Wilmington.

Groaning softly to herself, she tussled for a few moments with the ambiguous feelings.

If he didn't like her anymore, that was okay. For the last couple of weeks their relationship had been tenuous, to say the least. And why she had offered to take everyone to the Festival was beyond her. *I did tell them I would do it...I hate it when I make promises I don't really mean.*

Turning her attention toward the floats and little clown cars, she mustered a smile, then winced as she felt a drop of rain, then another on her skin. *Darn it, the weatherman said there was only going to be a twenty percent chance of rain today.*

She searched the crowd for Bell then noticed her only a few feet behind her.

Catching her gaze, Marla shrugged. "Guess it's going to twenty percent any minute."

Bell curled her upper lip and grunted, then held a bare arm out, testing the air for drops of rain. "I thought I felt something. I was hoping it was just a bird, but...nope, there goes one again." She pushed back against a stranger moving through the crowd and grabbed her boyfriend's hand. She and Pete retreated into the tiny alcove of a store front, she grunted another angry sigh.

Groans of discontentment rose from the people lining the sidewalks and streets, as the skies broke open. Immediately the crowd was moving in all directions. Some opened umbrellas, others pressed against store fronts, hoping to wait out the shower. Still others pushed their way through the throng of parade goers.

Abruptly, Marla and Jerry found themselves shoved into the small alcove with Pete and Bell.

Pete leaned into Bell and pulled his light jacket over his head, half shielding the girl from the progression of raindrops that had burst from the sky.

"I told you that it was going to rain today. But you wouldn't listen." He looked directly at Marla, and then wrapped an arm around Bell. She leaned in closer to the young man and flashed a disapproving look.

"So, where'd you park your car?" Pete asked, not bothering to hide his annoyance, his brow furrowing above his dark brown eyes.

"Yeah, where's your car?" Jerry echoed.

"I parked on Anne Street—about half way down on the right."

Pete nodded and grasped Bell's hand even tighter, pulling her along as they jogged toward the parked car.

Jerry's eyes hastily swept over Marla's face as he proceeded to follow the other two in the group, leaving her behind.

Marla sighed. Was she saddened because Jerry wasn't holding her hand and hurrying away to safety? No! She answered herself. She knew they were over. She'd known it for a while now—his actions today just cemented the fact and she found herself feeling not hurt, but indifferent. On the other hand, she did feel somewhat abandoned since she was the one who'd driven the group to the parade. She'd even dropped them off early and close to the festivities, then parked the car herself, walking back through the crowd to where she'd deposited the three twenty-somethings.

"Fool," she muttered, "some friends I've got." She moved slowly toward Anne Street, the rain pelting her short dark hair leaving it to drip into her eyes. She brushed the limp strands to the side of her face. "Why do I do this—try to be friends with people I really have nothing in common with? I just don't fit in—not with them anyway."

As she walked toward the car, Marla listened to the sounds of the crowd as it passed her by. Very few of the people were angry; she heard a few complaints, but not many. Most were laughing about getting caught in the rain or expressing sympathy for the people on floats or marching in bands.

As she neared Anne Street and her parked car, she noticed the fogged windows.

Didn't I lock my car? she thought as she approached the driver's side door. Marla looked curiously at the occupants as she opened it. All three were in the back seat. Looks of derision met her eyes. All but Pete quickly turned away; his sneer was defiant as if he was daring her to comment.

There was one thing Marla knew that Pete loved, and that was confrontation. She was not about to take the bait. She met his eyes, grinned, then cast her gaze toward Bell—whiny Bell hated confrontation.

"I used the spare key you gave me." The blond girl shrugged.

Marla shot her a heated stare, "If I remember correctly, I asked you to put that key back in the desk drawer after you borrowed my car a month ago."

"Oops, must have forgotten," Bell tittered.

"Hey, if she hadn't have had the key we would have been standing out there in the rain getting soaked waiting on your slow ass."

I could throw your ass out of my car and make you all walk home, Marla thought, but right now she did not feel like getting into it with Pete or with any of them. She just wanted to go home.

"Why?" she closed her eyes and whispered, reminding herself she had dug this hole and she was the only one who could get herself out of it. She held her hand out. "Keys–Now." Her eyes blazed into Bell's timid face.

True to form Bell began sniffling. Tears welled in her eyes. "I didn't mean–" She dug deep into her purse and handed the keys to Marla. "It's just that I haven't–"

"See what you did now," Jerry spat.

Same old crap, every time she gets caught with her hand in the cookie jar she starts crying, whining and it's always because of something else or somebody else–it's never her fault–she's always the victim.

Shaking her head, Marla guided the key into the ignition, checked her mirrors and fastened her seatbelt.

The rain was still coming down, but not nearly as steadily as before. She turned on the windshield wipers and slowly pulled away from the curb.

The trio in the back giggled and grunted. Marla felt Pete's knee in the back of her seat. Knowing he was aware of the discomfort he was causing, Marla looked in the rearview mirror–yes, he had that wicked sneer plastered on his face. Then she noticed Bell opening her purse wide and motioning for Pete to look inside. They both nodded.

Marla sighed lightly, and thought *What are they up to?* She refused to engage in an argument with him. Rather, she moved ahead slowly to the stop sign.

Looking both ways, she grinned, noticing a family of four—mother, father, son and daughter—all holding hands and laughing as the rain soaked them. They seemed delighted with the wetness as they splashed in the roadside puddles.

As they crossed the street, Marla pulled forward and drove another block to another stop sign. Here there were no people and very little traffic. She looked to the right and then to the left. And then she saw him.

He stood on the edge of the curb, his brown eyes looking directly into hers.

"Poor doggy," she heard herself say aloud. Opening the window, she looked more closely at the dog. He seemed so scared and lonely.

"Hey! Don't you dare let that damn dog in this car." Pete ordered.

If he hadn't have said it with such vehemence. If he hadn't have been so cruel and disdainful ever since she'd known him—maybe she wouldn't have done it.

But the instant the last syllable left his wretched lips, Marla opened the door and patted her thigh. "Come on boy, come on."

Without delay the little dog hopped on her lap. She could feel his wet paws through her jeans.

"Damn stinking dog," Jerry scoffed.

Now he speaks up. Sniveling little minion. What in the world did I ever see in him?

She reached her hand to ruffle the little dog's fur and felt the thin strip of a leather collar around his neck. Thinking that perhaps she should pull over and check the collar for a name or address, Marla glanced into the rearview mirror. Bell had her hand cupped to Pete's ear and was whispering something. Jerry was leaning in as closely as he could, hoping to catch a word.

On second thought, I don't think I'll pull over right now. I kind of like the company of this little dog. She looked down again and entwined her fingers in the damp hair. Reaching up, the dog licked Marla's cheek.

A low groan emanated from the back seat. "That makes me sick. You don't know where that dog has been. And you don't know what else he's been licking," Pete complained.

Taking a quick look in the rearview mirror, Marla caught Pete's eyes. He glared at her before leaning into Bell's whisper.

"The dog is going to ruin everything," the blonde girl murmured too loudly.

"Huh?" Marla looked in the rearview mirror. "Ruin what?"

"Nothing!" Pete growled, "you must be hearing things." He shot an explosive look of contempt to Marla as she pressed on the gas and moved forward.

Suddenly the backseat was quiet.

The hint of a grin settled on her lips as she drove along the streets, turning finally at tenth street and then onto Market. Still the backseaters hadn't said a word.

"Think I'll pull over at this gas station and check out this puppy's collar. Maybe there is an address."

In the rearview she caught the scornful expressions of the three passengers. Pete grumbled something; Jerry adding unintelligible words to the furtive conversation.

Bell sat busy with her hands in her purse scrounging for something or other.

"Here it is," Marla exclaimed. "Tupper. His name is Tupper."

"Tupperware?" Pete guffawed, "That's a stupid name.

"I didn't say Tupperware. I said Tupper. Just plain Tupper."

"It's still stupid," added Jerry.

Now, what would Jerry say if I told him he was stupid? Would Pete stand up for him or would he agree with me? Pondering the questions, Marla surmised that if she did say anything about Jerry's intelligence it would just start a row. *It's just not worth it.*

Rubbing her thumb across the dirt-encrusted name tag again; she could barely make out an address—406 Lightning Rod Lane. She spoke it aloud. "Four O Six Lightning Rod Lane."

"Where's that?" Bell asked timidly.

"Hey! I just want to get home." Pete snarled. "We've spent all day in the rain and riding around with a smelly dog. The whole day's been wasted."

"Yeah." Jerry hissed, then added an exaggerated groan.

Jerry was laughable, she was laughable. A feeling of disgust settled in her belly as she recalled letting him kiss her. *Oh geez, why did I do that?*

Feeling nausea rise, she calmed herself, kept her composure and searched the phone for the GPS app and punched in the address.

Lightning Rod Lane was six and a half miles from where she was now parked. She thought of mentioning this to her passengers but decided not to.

Sliding into drive, she pulled out into the steady flowing traffic and proceeded toward her destination.

By now, Tupper had settled himself in the front passenger seat. Occasionally Marla would reach a hand to stroke his thick fur. *Kind of looks like a Lhasa Apso.* She thought. *He's black and white and has that little beard they are known for.*

Tupper wagged his tail as Marla looked at him and grinned.

He sure is a long way from home, she thought. *He must be lost or maybe his owner just didn't want him.*

Another glance in the back seat reassured Marla's conviction that she trusted this strange dog much more than she trusted the strangers in the back seat.

And that's who they were—strangers. Why she
had ever believed they were friends was beyond
her.

Marla's thoughts drifted back to the day she'd
met Bell. It was at the bank. She'd gone in to make
the weekly deposit for Eastern Boat Works—her
business—hers now. With her father's passing, she
was now the sole owner.

And oh how she missed her father. They'd been
close, spending most of her waking hours either at
his shop or on the water—fishing, diving, skiing. She
had loved it all. Her father's unexpected death had
been a shock.

She shrugged and drew her lips into a line, as
she thought warmly of her deceased father. He had
died too young.

Maybe his passing had made her lonely—who
knew?

Bell had been a quiet person when Marla first
met her; her light blue eyes begged for friendship
and Marla had the heart that couldn't say no. *The
girl needs a friend, I need a friend*, she told herself
and after bumping into her over and over again at
the grocery store or pharmacy, it just seemed
natural to develop a friendship.

Sometimes Bell had Pete on her arm when she saw her about town. He seemed a nice enough guy—a little standoffish though. Marla was never quite comfortable with him. But she'd overlooked the discomfort when Bell mentioned that it took a while for Pete to warm up to people—it was just his way.

Marla reached to pet Tupper once again. The look in his eyes this time was different—maybe forlorn. *Yes, that's it—but why?*

Maybe he doesn't want to go home. As soon as the thought entered her mind she considered what it would be like to take the little dog to her house and just keep him as her own.

"Two miles, then turn left on Cumberland Road," a soft voice spoke from the GPS.

She thought about the possibility of keeping Tupper and glanced at the dog again. *You want to come home with me?* Marla dared not say the words aloud.

But as if the dog had heard her, its ears perked up and its tail wagged.

Shaking her head, Marla whispered. "That would be stealing." Instantly the dog's ears drooped and he rested his head on his paws.

Marla's thoughts returned to when she first met Bell, Pete and Jerry.

Yeah, Pete was always a little demanding. But he was Bell's boyfriend and none of my business and then she talked me into meeting Jerry.

As she drove, Marla rolled her eyes. *Geez, what an idio*t. She held back a laugh, realizing that not only was she an idiot for dating him, but he really was an idiot.

He doesn't have a single thought of his own that isn't put there by his Pete. She sighed as she contemplated the young man's physique. *But he does look good. He could be another George Clooney. He's just dumb as a sack of hammers.*

Twice he'd asked to borrow money from her. She obliged him the first time. But when she declined the second—that was it. That was when he started acting distant.

Marla took another quick look in the rearview mirror. All three-heads were bowed as they held their phones, texting.

She studied their expressions. Jerry looked pensive, serious—his mouth was pursed.

Pete's lips were curled upward at the corners and Bell's mouth hung open as she moved her thumbs quickly across the keyboard of her phone.

It's about me, she shrugged. *They're texting nasty things about me.*

"Turn right at Border Street." The words from the GPS startled her for a moment.

She thought of the words her father always spoke, 'You don't have to be friends with everyone, just be nice. Take care of yourself before you try saving the world.'

Bell and her group felt wrong–her father had always told her to go with her gut and her gut kept telling her no–no about Bell, no about Jerry and an emphatic no about Pete. There was just something–and it didn't feel right.

Tupper stood in the seat and wagged his tail. His tongue, hanging from his jaw, dripped a few drops of saliva.

"That's nasty," Jerry spat.

It was hot in the car and very humid outside. Marla reached to turn on the air conditioner. Ordinarily she would have rolled the windows down on a seventy degree day. But with the rain, the A/C would have to do.

The little dog released a tiny yap, and it pranced in the seat. Placing his paws once again on her thighs, he licked her cheek.

"What is it boy?" Grinning, Marla spoke playfully to the dog.

"Stupid dog is nuts, you're going to catch something from that mutt." Pete spoke the words commandingly, as if he was an authority on dogs. But of course, Pete had always acted as if he knew it all.

His parents didn't have to waste any money on college for him, he already knows everything. Marla chuckled to herself.

"What are you laughing about?" Jerry interjected angrily.

"She's not going to be laughing—" Bell sneered.

Pete jabbed Bell in her side with his elbow and pursed his mouth. He said something under his breath. Marla stretched to hear the words, but had no luck.

What's going on? Instantly a sense of discomfort swept through Marla; she focused on the road ahead, feeling her heart pounding rapidly in her chest.

Now she felt even more uncomfortable with the three people in the backseat. A chill ran through her. *Maybe that's the A/C,* she thought quickly to herself, but no, there was something else. Glancing once again into the mirror, she noticed the hard stares of her passengers.

Tupper whined, then growled.

"Turn right at the next intersection," the GPS sounded. Marla pulled into the right lane and waited for a car to pass.

"Turn right at Lightning Rod Lane and proceed one half mile."

Obeying the GPS, Marla pulled onto a narrow dirt road and drove as an ominous silence filled the car.

"You are now at four o six Lightning Rod Lane." The words from the GPS soothed Marla as she pulled in front of a nearly obscured structure surrounded by old oaks whose limbs hung touching the ground. Spanish moss dripped like earrings from the branches.

The rain had stopped; a hazy mist enveloped the air.

Marla spied the tiny blue cottage that sat nearly hidden among the thick rambling greenery intertwined with wisteria. Its pungent aroma draped the scene as the whirring of dragonflies clouded the yard and surrounding area.

Nervously reaching for the car's door handle the frightened girl opened it; she and Tupper bounded out.

Expecting the dog to run to the front door, Marla was puzzled when Tupper reached his front paws to her thighs and barked loudly.

Was it the tingling chill of early spring, the breeze, the rain? Goose bumps raised, it seemed, on her entire body. Her breath came quickly and for a moment she felt dizzy.

There was no reason to be afraid. Was there? Not out here—out of the car where she had felt the meneacing presence of her three companions.

She studied her surroundings. They were foreign. Were they welcoming?

Turning to watch the others slowly exit the car, Marla turned to the little blue cottage for solace and gradually walked toward the door.

Uneven cobblestones unbalanced her gait as she stepped carefully. She could hear mutterings from the three behind her, but she wasn't about to stop and ask them what they were saying.

Nothing felt right. Nothing felt safe, except for the little dog Tupper and the hope that perhaps behind the wooden door was safety. Marla tapped lightly on it, it swung open a bit. Tupper pushed even farther with his nose and stood looking up at Marla as if to invite her in.

"You're not going in that house, are you?" called Bell.

Marla pushed the door open farther, and walked across the threshold. It was nearly dark inside. A taxidermied snake, perched on an end table, seemed to hiss at her. A dusty red fox stared at her blankly from a side wall. Turning, she saw Pete, Jerry and Bell; they had stopped, their backs turned to her—heads lowered as they spoke in undertones. Pete's eyes rose quickly to meet hers.

What was it? Now they were all looking at her with the same threatening emanations radiating from them.

Marla walked farther into the cottage, calling out, "Hello? Hello. Is anyone home? I found your dog. Tupper—your little black and white dog. Did you lose your dog?"

There was no response.

Looking back at the people she'd driven with, Marla watched as Pete spewed a line of spit toward a bush.

"There's no one here," she heard him say. His face twisted into a broad grin as he raised his head to glare at her again.

She could have sworn she heard him add, "We've got to do it today." She eyed the other two companions; their eyes avoided hers.

Jerry attempted to spit a stream toward the vinery, but the dribble fell against his chin.

He raised a bare arm to wipe it away.

Bell, her mouth still hanging open, once again was searching through her oversized purse.

Marla saw her head jerk to listen to Pete.

"Huh? But she..."

"Shut your freaking mouth, she'll hear you."

Marla heard the stifled bit of conversation, then watched as they drew into a huddle once again and began whispering.

"So there you are!" A grainy sounding voice pierced the silence; a tall older woman—maybe in her sixties—came from behind a partition. She snapped her fingers at the dog.

"Where did you go this time?" She eyed the dog scornfully, then winked. "What have you been up to now?"

Feeling her chest rise and fall, Marla gulped a breath before speaking. "He was downtown—at the parade—it was raining—I—let him in my car."

The woman pulled her shoulders erect—her thin chin squared as she ran long yellowed nails near the sides of her face to catch the stray strands of hair and settle them back into the bun at the nape of her neck.

She sucked in air, released a heavy sigh and lifted her head higher; she seemed to grow another few inches in doing so. Smoothing the skirt of her long gray dress she slid a glance from the dog to Marla and back again.

"He always did like pretty young things." Moving closer, the older woman picked at a spot on her dress, one of many.

Some sort of stain, thought Marla. She eyed the thick cloth of the dress, it had many stains. *She must be hot in that heavy material*, Marla reflected.

"I know, it's hot. This dress is hot and it is muggy and humid outside." She bent to reach her bony fingers to Tupper's muzzle.

Gingerly he smelled them, then looked up into the woman's eyes.

"See? See what you missed?"

Perplexed, Marla stuttered, "I'm uh–just bringing–"

"Not to worry, my dear. I have been fixing a late lunch in the kitchen and Tupper loves tongue." She raised her head and winked, "Tongue sandwich. Would you like one?"

Unconsciously crinkling her nose, Marla shook her head, "No thank you, Ma'am."

"And I see you have friends with you," The woman leaned to the side and studied the people standing outside her doorway. "Are these your friends?"

The intensity of the woman's green eyes took Marla's breath away and she felt herself gasp for air.

"These are not your friends. Are they, my dear?" The woman lowered her eyes and whispered garbled words.

"Well, we came to the parade together," Marla answered nervously.

Holding the skirt of her dress to the side, the woman swept by Marla.

A sharp pop and crack echoed in the thick spring air as the older woman passed by. Marla watched as she stretched a long cloth covered arm against the sash of the doorway.

"I see you..." The words seemed blown through a tunnel. "My name is Decebal Caine." The wind raised as she spoke; tendrils of the woman's hair blew from her tight bun.

Long bony fingers pulled strips of cloth from the hair where it had become matted. She threw them to the ground.

"Do you not hear me? I am Decebal Caine!"

Pete looked toward Decebal, he squinted his eyes, then raised his hands above them as if the sun was glaring. Pulling his lips inward, he cast a repentant gaze toward Marla.

Jerry stepped forward toward the door where Decebal stood. "Tuh, puh," he began. "Tuh puh!" His mouth gaped; his hands flew to cover it.

Bell, inched along the cobbled steps toward the door as well. "Huh?" Losing her balance she stumbled, scraping her knee. The contents of her purse spilled out onto the ground. Quickly she reached a hand to retrieve a long bladed knife and scoot it back inside the faux leather bag.

A puzzled expression covered her face as she attempted to speak, "Tuh, tuh, tuh." She reached her hand inside her mouth, "Awww, uuuh," Her eyes widened aghast with horror; tears flowed down her cheeks as she turned to look at Marla, the dog and the old woman.

"Cat got your tongue?" Decebal Caine asked snidely, her eyes glaring; the long nails of her hands drawing slowly about her chin and lips.

Pete screamed what seemed to be the word 'no.' He repeated it again and again, pointing at the little black and white dog. "Duh dahg aht it!" He looked angrily from the old woman to Marla and then to the dog.

"Can't understand a word the boy says," Decebal cackled. Turning to Marla she caught the wisps of hair that had strayed from her bun and pushed them back in place, "I still have those sandwiches in the kitchen," the old woman spoke sternly. "Tupper loves tongue."

The little dog stood in the doorway, his tail wagging. He barked happily and led the way back into the house and its safety.

Featured Author

Dee Dee Paliotti Lloyd

Dee Dee Palioti Lloyd is a native of Topsail. She grew up on the island in the 1950s, 60s, and beyond. A curious and brave girl, Dee Dee was and is an exemplary pirate at heart.

She is and always has been her own person–one who speaks her mind–a rare characteristic–one to be respected.

The following poem is by Dee Dee. It captures those days of the young native islanders when the island was young too.

BARNACLE BILL'S

by Dee Dee Paliotti Lloyd

When I was young, I used to go
To a place on the beach you might know.
A place where friends
would always meet,
To share a soda or get something to eat.
The Corner Booth was the place to sit,
Sometimes we raced our friends to get it.
I know it was stupid
but that was our will
My younger days at Barnacle Bill's.

Walk out on 'The Back Deck' if you dare,
For only "The Cool" hung out there.
Surfers on their boards
waiting for a wave,
Often saving swimmers from
their watery grave.
Everyday we experienced a new first,
Laughing so hard, we thought we'd burst.
I often think and
wish for those days still,
The sweet memories of Barnacle Bill's.

Friends hid friends
from their angry mom and dad
We consoled each other when
we were sad.
Where we crossed our hearts
and hoped to die,
Where we got Triple Dog Dare
to talk to a cute guy.
Pinky promises were made
and never broken
Feelings of love were often unspoken.
To have those days back I would
almost kill,
To go back to the days of Barnacle Bill's.

Where Marcy and I found a
pack of cigarettes
Lit them behind the dunes, we did regret.
This was the spot, when we
snuck out at night,
Try to make it home before it got light.
Tricks on tourists were always fun
to play,
Yelling SHARK! then running away.
Riding our bikes down that big hill,
Those crazy days at Barnacle Bill's.

If we were angels, which was
never our desire,
We'd all have crooked halos and
one wing in the fire.
Walking on the pier to see what was caught,
Sitting at the end, staring…
in deep thought.
Every time we got together it was a thrill,
Those good old times at Barnacle Bill's.

Featured Author

Diane Batts Geary

Diane Batts Geary was the first permanent child resident in Surf City. She was two years old when she came to the island in 1948. She remembers what our burgeoning little town was like before "the secret was out."

Each of us who grew up here held a sense of ownership—the island was our place—untouched and unsullied by the rest of the world.

Diane's love for Topsail is immeasurable. I find her wise, caring, and practical. She is who I go to when I need a really good dose of the way it used to be.

GROWING UP

ON TOPSAIL ISLAND

by Diane Batts Geary

In 1948 the operation Bumble Bee and Camp Davis people had all left the island. It reverted back to the original owners. My daddy, Roland Batts, was one of them.

Between he and his five brothers and two sisters the Batts family owned around five hundred acres on the island.

Daddy had a dream to live on the island and help develop it. My momma was not too keen on the idea. But Daddy persisted.

There were already several buildings on the island, all left there by the Army and Navy. There were several barracks, an officer's club, a few out fire stations, horse stables.

One of the fire houses had one big room and bath in the back and in the front was a big open bay. That's where we first moved to when we came to the island.

My father wanted to open a small market there with sodas, milk, bread, canned goods and other grocery items. Momma said, "no way."

At that time she was in her late forties and had a comfortable home in Sneads Ferry. I was only two at the time and I think Momma wanted to raise her youngest child in a familiar setting.

Daddy said, 'okay' to her as he put the cooking stove in the back of his truck. He picked me up and put me in the truck too.

Momma said, "okay," once more and then she got into the truck as well.

Well, there we were on a barren island with only a few fishing shacks and fishermen who came now and then.

But Daddy had a dream. "Momma, he said, "One day this place will be full of families who want to live here and fish. It will be a good outlet for the farmers who want to come here and spend their money after the tobacco season.

Time went by and sure enough, the fishermen did come. The farmers and a few came after their farming season and a few military families from Camp Lejeune in Jacksonville moved over here too.

Even some of the big names from Jacksonville came with their wives and children to enjoy the summer months and weekends.

Those summer months were when store owners and people who rented made their money. In the winter, when the rich and distinctive families left, things got really tight.

In Daddy's own words, "some of the groceries spoiled from lack of customers."

I was not aware of any of this. My mind was on my German Shepard, Rusty and playmates.

Rusty and I played across the street from Daddy's store in the hot sand. When I was tired and hot we went into the store where Momma would give me two ice cream sticks. I ate mine while I held the other one for Rusty to eat.

Eventually a military family would move in with a child or children close to my age. So then I had playmates, but they usually didn't stay long. The fathers were shipped out to somewhere else.

By the time I started first grade my Dad had built a two story block building across the street. The down stairs had a small grocery store and post office on one side and a small café on the other. Daddy said he wanted a café so the fishermen had more to eat than sardines, Vienna sausage, cheese and crackers.

During my elementary school years I played in the sand and walked the beach looking for shells. I spent a lot of time with my German Shepard dog, Rusty. We often sat in the dunes and had tea parties.

I had cousins that lived on the mainland and when they came to the island we played in the sand dunes running up and down. We broke off sea oats and pretended we were fighting off pirates. The last person standing at the top of the dune became King of the Hill.

While on the dunes we once saw a man going into my Dad's store, he had long hair and a long black beard. We hid behind the dunes thinking this was Blackbeard himself.

My mother was a very hospitable woman. Everyone who came to her door was invited to come in and have a biscuit and a cup of coffee.

So being her daughter, the hospitality gene was passed on to me. Sometimes one of the local boys would come by to my "sand pit," as my mother called it; there I would invite him in to my imaginary house to have lunch. On my imaginary stove I would have sand soup made from sand and water and my special sand biscuits. Now to make these, I had to mix sand and water–flatten out the little patties and bake them in the sun–voila! I had biscuits.

By Junior high I was more interested in crabbing under the swing bridge and once in a while, defying Momma's instructions, I would go to the pier where I was challenged by the local boys to sit on the cross bars under the pier to see how long I could sit there before being knocked off by a wave.

Well, you had to find the entertainment where you could. The old Bumble Bee towers were another favorite spot. We would climb the old rickety stairs and look out over the ocean waves to see if we could see the tall pirate ships we thought were out there.

By high school my mind was set going to the big city. On the island, people from bigger name cities like Fayetteville, Raleigh, Charlotte, came to visit. Many stayed the whole summer and left when school started back. To me they were going back to their beautiful home and city life. It had to be better than Topsail.

My family didn't go to visit places like big cities. We were what was called, land poor. We made our living during the summer months when tourists from other places came to visit and in the fall when fishermen and their families rented here on the island. So, while I lived under my parent's roof, I never did get to see anything other than the island.

I did get to go to the big city after I graduated from high school. There I went downtown–I remember a popular tune at the time by Petula Clark. It was called "Downtown" and it spoke of the bright lights and the music of the traffic–a place where you could forget your troubles.

It was a pretty song, but after a couple of years in the big city, I decided that downtown was not what I was looking for.

My father had died my last year in high school, my elderly mother was ill and I wanted to go home where I could smell the salt air, hear the roar of the waves caressing the beach and where I knew every neighbor by name.

If you were not around in the fifties and sixties, you missed the allure of a small community where young people could have a bonfire on the beach in late evenings.

We didn't have a movie theater or bowling alley. We made our own fun from what God gave us.

Sometimes a group of us would go on a scavenger hunt. We'd go from house to house looking for a pin or a button of a certain color. Sometimes we'd get the mayor's autograph.

Parents didn't worry about the kids on the beach. Everyone looked out for each other.

Life on the island has changed. Progress they call it now.

Do I think my father would be proud of the island's progress? No, his vision was a fishing village where every man could afford to come and vacation.

At the corner of New River Drive and Topsail Drive there used to be a sign, "R.T. Batts Welcomes You to the Fisherman's Paradise."

Introduction

The following is an essay written several years ago, after a long absence from Topsail. I would like to say that I have reconciled myself to the many changes that have occurred in the last several years, but I cannot.

I still love my island, despite those changes, and for those of us who were fortunate enough to have the Topsail experience in our youth, we know we had the best—the best of the island.

MY ISLAND NO MORE

I studied the old aerial photograph once more as I paused at the red light. It would not be long, maybe half an hour or so before I would be at Topsail Island, the home of my childhood.

Smiling, I eased my foot from the brake and moved through traffic, images of my youth spent climbing dunes and racing to the ocean danced in my head, expanding, animating. I saw myself on the island as a child dancing along the shore, running, diving into the waves, climbing mountains of sand, riding my bike along the sparsely populated roadways, picking wild grasses that bloomed in the dune valleys.

I had been away for twenty years. Anticipation of a simpler life and time flooded my mind as the clunkety clunk of the old swing bridge passed beneath my car. I was home!

Rather than the joy of familiarity greeting me, only remnants of that simpler time stared back. Things had changed.

"Where did you go?" the island and I seemed to say to one another.

I could feel the breaking of my heart as I slowly drove in disbelief along the main road. Pretentious wooden hulks towered in places where voluptuous dunes, standing stories tall, had once been.

Windswept oaks and merkle bushes had been ripped from their sandy soil to provide room for tropical palms and pampas grass.

These were not indigenous to this coast.

They glared arrogantly as if to say, "*Real beaches grow us.*" I shook my head at the ostentatious flora.

The quaint and subtle beauty was gone. Perhaps if I had not been away for so long the change would not have been so shocking. Then again, I thought, if I had not been away would this have happened? But who am I? Merely a follower, standing back only to enjoy the benefits of God's handiwork, never a mover and shaker. How much of a fight would I have put up against "progress"?

Structure after structure gawked at me from the bulldozed dunes populated with hand sown sea oats. I heard their rustle as a light breeze kicked up. SHE was always coy—*I still have this*—the island seemed to say.

I parked my car and made my way up the forbidden man-made dunes–small renditions–ugly attempts at the natural.

Warning signs jutted from them intermittently, in large bright letters they blared, DO NOT TOUCH. But they had already been destroyed.

The oats waved staunchly among the dunes, bravely even, midst blotches of planted grasses that gapped like implants on a bald man's head.

Where was the blue stem and yucca? I saw a couple where dozens should have been, but their home was gone. The dune valleys and troughs had disappeared as had my beloved hairawn muhly–not one from stem to stern of the island did I find.

Then I felt it in my belly, the taking of my island. Like a once vibrant smooth skinned girl, she had been taken by force. The feeling was raw and wrenching. She had been deceived by those who loved her, or said they did. She was plied with trinkets and promises–*you will be even more beautiful, so many people will come to see you*–low words of love and lies that forced her trust, her belief, her all–caressing her as they ripped across her center and smashed her heart.

The vast expanses of oaks, merkles, sand spurs and the valley troughs, all while cooing, "I will always take care of you."

"Oh my heart, my heart," I moaned, falling to my knees. "What have they done to you?" My feet sank into the fragile sliding sand of the man-made dunes and I made my way back to the water to rinse the coarseness from my body. Then I saw a glimpse of the beauty peeking out from a vacant lot of sand spurs and spiny cactus, who warned futilely beside the metal sign proclaiming a fine for trespassing.

Like a princess wearing a faded formal gown, She whispered, "Listen."

The steady roar of the ocean and the sand as it roiled with the wind gusts spoke in desperation of the lost dignity and grace. Wrapped in the gossamer blur of sand, I felt her wretchedness from the deception and exploitation. It had left her a jaded entity.

"Listen," She whispered again. I listened for bits and pieces of that long gone past and in my soul I heard her more clearly, as I watched a ghost crab scuttle to its hole home. Empty rental properties gaped at me as if to dissuade me, but still I listened—closing my eyes to their glare.

101

"Yes, I am no longer what I once was, but I exist. Even with all this." A sigh of breeze and a gust of diaphanous sand rolled across the beach. "There are those who say I'm still beautiful."

I thought how low their standards must be and I called back, "What is more beautiful, a bare dune, softly rounded by time's hand with all the indigenous vegetation, or a million dollar painted house standing where that once was?"

She paused, sighed as the breeze, then tittered back, "I know, but what's a girl to do?" The pain of her loss fell as ocean mist on my arms, then I heard a soft echo reply. "You have what they don't–you remember." A rogue wave crashed loudly at the shore as I recalled yellow mornings and red nights, the laughter of my pirate friends as we chased each other through the sand mountains, the uneasiness of sand in my swimsuit.

Foam-tipped sea water caressed my toes and the voice breezed through my hair, the roiling sand subsiding.

"In time I will be whole again. In time these spoiled sands will regain what is theirs, the palms will die, the rest that doesn't belong here will die too and the massive wooden structures will be claimed by My Sister, the Sea. In time I'll be back."

Yes, in time, I thought–ambiguous a resolution as it was. "In time, I'll be gone," I laughed aloud.

"But you'll know, you'll see. Be patient."

I sat at the shore as I had as a child and let the water pool around my legs. The waves ebbed back and forth bringing swirling sand.

Nodding, and with my back to the hulks, I gazed out into the ocean.

BRENDA

Coming of Age

In 1965 Brenda was new to the island. She lived, along with her father, in a little white house a block or so from the Surf City Baptist church.

Rumor had it that her mother had passed away, but no one was sure. Neither Brenda nor her father talked much about that.

Her father was a military man, a Marine from Camp Lejeune in Jacksonville.

My father was a retired Navy Corpsman, so I was familiar with military living and how sometimes it made you feel different or not accepted as one of the locals, even though in 1965 my family had been living on the island for ten years.

Now, I consider that Brenda had it doubly hard, moving into a new place—a new town—and coming into womanhood with no mother.

But then, at twelve years old, I didn't consider those things and I looked at Brenda as just another kid to play with.

Back then there were few playmates on the island and when a new kid came to town (the military transients came and left every year or so) it was a real treat.

Since she lived practically next door to me, Brenda and I struck up a friendship. I was tickled pink, since she was the only girl on the island that was in the same grade as I.

We'd ride the thirteen miles to school in Hampstead sitting together on the bus, in the same seat, helping each other with homework and giggling about one thing or another—just being kids.

I guess we had a lot in common: we were the same age, were in the same grade and both our fathers were military men.

It was nice having someone so much like me.

Perhaps it was because of my father's youth (he was thirty-nine when he retired) or maybe it was simply his character. But my father was not nearly as strict and gruff as Brenda's.

I recall her father barking orders and scowling at his daughter—standing over her as she busied herself with a task.

He'd run a finger over areas where she had cleaned to see if they measured up and peer closely at the mirrors to see if they were streak-less.

I remember one particular day, waiting for Brenda to complete a task. She simply could not meet her father's requirements and so she re-did it over and over again.

She never cried or shed a tear as she attempted to make things perfect, rather her determination to please him burned in an angry glare.

My father never did those things. He never harped at me or ridiculed me. Daddy instructed me once, as matter of factly as he could, and that was the end of it. If I did not meet his standards, I was punished by losing accolades for a job well done. And those were prized accolades.

Daddy never struck me nor yelled at me. That was Momma's job.

But Brenda had no mother, no one to ease the relationship between daughter and father. And Brenda's father was as gruff as he would have been with his own Marines on base. Or so it seemed.

Through the summer months, Brenda and I played in the ocean on big truck-sized inner tubes and walked to Barnacle Bill's Fishing Pier to go fishing or just be around other kids visiting with their families from other little southern towns in North Carolina.

Parents did that back then–let the beach children off the leash, so to speak–everyone looked out for the other's children and most of us minded the instructions our parents gave us before letting us out the door.

We had lots of fun, rolling down the big sand dunes toward the ocean–jumping in the water to get wet, then racing back up the dune to roll back down and get all sandy again. This was repeated and repeated–it was fun.

There were towers to climb, the ones left by Operation Bumble Bee from the late 1940s, and then there was the old warehouse where abandoned military vehicles from World War II provided all sorts of interesting scenarios for curious young minds. We climbed on them, into them, pretended we were soldiers, hid under them–all sorts of things.

Compared to today, it was amazing how much fun we children had outdoors–but we did.

There were three two-story sand dunes in my backyard and seeing that Brenda's home and mine were so close together, Brenda and I often played together there.

I was very much into horses at the time. I'd heard from my father, who grew up in Texas, how as a boy he spent most of his waking hours riding his horse Topsy. And then there were Saturday morning cartoons with Fury, The Lone Ranger and his horse Silver, Roy Rogers and his horse Trigger, then Mr. Ed on television at night. I'm sure with all the horse shows on TV. I wasn't the only little girl who wanted one.

I read all the popular horse books of the day and imagined having a horse of my own to ride up and down the sand dunes.

I read everything about horses, even looking them up in the encyclopedia where I found their prehistoric cousin, eohippus.

Eohippus was small, about the size of a small to medium sized dog.

One night as I was walking home from church and passing by the row of trash cans beyond my home, I spied small creatures scurrying about.

To my horse-loving filled imagination, I was certain that those creatures were eohippus. I ran to tell Daddy, who chuckled, then found another picture in the encyclopedia of a rat, he explained the similarity.

I was crestfallen. However, I wanted to believe Daddy was wrong; I clung to the romance of little horses outside my door.

I can't remember if Brenda was as much a horse enthusiast as I was; nevertheless, she indulged me and we would play as horses on the big sand dunes in my back yard.

She was always the Black Stallion, I was Man-O-War, and we raced up and down the dunes whinnying and snorting as powerful horses do. We reared up on our hind legs and fought—our arms outstretched pawing at the air.

We played horsey games throughout the summer and into the early fall when after school and homework, we would race to the dunes again to pretend.

Pretending is a big deal in adolescence—I think it comes with the territory. I was lost in a world of horses and pirates and my dogs. Other stuff, like boys, teased hair and make-up, were just not on my radar screen—not yet.

Over the winter, we both turned another year older. Still, Brenda and I met occasionally on the dunes to play, but I didn't see her as often. It seemed her father always had her busy doing something or other.

We still sat together on the school bus, though she was quieter than she had been those early months when I had first met her. But most of the time she declined my request to play horses in the backyard.

One day, on the way home from school, she asked me, "Why don't we sneak out of the house tonight?"

I know my eyes must have grown to saucer size, because I was aghast at the suggestion. At that time I did nothing without my parent's permission. I'd been taught that only *bad* children lie and do sneaky things.

But I admired Brenda so, that I told her I would and we spent the remainder of the ride home discussing when and where to meet.

Both of our fathers were early risers. Her father had to be at Camp Lejeune by six a.m. and my father opened his gas station at the same time. They both went to bed relatively early.

I felt very guilty about deceiving my father. I had always looked up to him and endeavored to never disappoint him—that was worse than a spanking from my mother. But my guilt did not deter me and so at twelve o'clock, midnight, I sneaked out of my bedroom, opened the back door and waited for Brenda to meet me.

I thought that she and I would probably go and climb one of the towers, or maybe go to Barnacle Bill's–the fishing pier was open all night long.

I didn't think that we would engage in sin. I wasn't interested in sin at that time and had no idea that Brenda was.

Within a few minutes of waiting at my back door, Brenda showed up.

"Come on," she whispered as she beckoned with her long arms.

I looked at her; she seemed different in some way. Her eyes sparkled, her hair was unkempt and tittering laughter bubbled from her lips.

Her feet were bare, and she wore a long flowing blouse that, in the night breeze, billowed about her.

The short white skirt she wore shone nearly florescent against her long tanned legs and she ran as she called for me to follow her.

And I did follow her, somewhat reluctantly, but still, I followed to where she finally stopped. I was perplexed at her choice–the Baptist church. We entered the unlocked doors.

It smelled new and clean. The moon shone lightly through the paned windows, exposing the red carpet between the aisles of pews.

They were blond pine pews, sanded and lacquered smooth and they led to the little altar at the front of the church.

In Remembrance of Me was etched into the wood of the altar.

I remembered how several years before, a young girl child had been laid atop that altar. She was beautiful, my age, blond and so very young. It was all so sad those many years ago.

I hesitated at the memory; it felt so wrong to be in that church, and for what? Why had Brenda chosen to come here? She never came to church at all.

My family was not big churchgoers either; both parents worked Sundays and my older brother and sister were gone from home by the time I was a teen.

But I usually went to Sunday School. I liked it. I loved hearing about Jesus and his kindness and love.

As I pondered the whys of being there, Brenda began to dance. The white skirt she wore flared as she twirled and swayed. Taking long light steps on her toes, she leapt and spun slowly.

As her eyes closed, a faint smile came to her lips; she tip-toed again, twirled again and reached a hand into the corners of the room where the moonlight did not shine.

Quickly she pulled her hand back and wrapped her arms around her body, her head lowered and she moved back into the darkness with a measured twirl, then back into the light to lift her arms above her, pulling them slowly to her chest.

I stood near the last pew, close to the door and watched her dance. I listened to her whispered laughter and nearly silent moans.

"Why don't you dance with me?" She asked without stopping.

I tried to join in, but my movements could not match her fluidity. I felt awkward—uncomfortable. Soon I retreated back into the shadows to watch her as she continued floating about. And her body, slowly, through ritual-like steps, began a dance more close to the earth.

She knelt on the carpet, moving her waist and shoulders from side to side, making a small circle. Her eyes closed. She rolled her head from side to side and hummed a sorrowful tune.

Brenda touched the carpet with her hands, bowing her head almost to the floor and then swiftly she brought her entire body to an erect position.

As a finale, she did cartwheels down the aisle and back again, ending in a split in front of the altar.

"What do you want to do now?" I blurted out. Brenda did not answer me.

"We better go," She said. "If my father caught me—"

That was the only time I sneaked out of my house to be with Brenda.

As summer neared and school let out for vacation, I saw her less and less. She no longer wanted to play in the dunes behind my house.

My feelings were hurt and I didn't understand why she did not want to be my friend anymore. What had I done?

That summer my family and I went on a long vacation traveling about the country, we came back a few weeks before school started. I still had not seen Brenda.

The first day of school came and I walked up the little steps of the bus and settled myself in a seat halfway between the front and back.

Anticipating the next stop—Brenda's—I looked for my friend as the doors of the bus opened.

This girl, yes, she was Brenda, but she had changed. Her hair was teased and fixed just so, with a curl in front of each ear. She wore eye liner and eye shadow.

Her short skirt came way above her knees and her blouse—oh, her blouse! Brenda had grown breasts—big ones.

She glanced my way, nodded and grinned politely, then sat with an older boy three seats in front of me.

Reaching his arm around her, Brenda leaned into him, and looking into each other's eyes, they kissed.

I know now that Brenda had been in transition those last months of our friendship.

She was becoming a woman and without a mother to guide her, it must have been a difficult journey. I surely did not understand Brenda's changing at all.

Me—I still played with my dog and loved reading about horses for several more years.

PLUM DUFF

A little dessert

"Hey." Leaning to the side, Bob nudged his wife gently on the arm.

Marylou raised her eyes from the book she held and looked above her reading glasses. "Huh?" she asked sheepishly.

"That was a good pot roast you made for dinner tonight." Her husband grinned, then inched a bit closer. "You want some dessert?" He raised his eyebrows and grinned more broadly.

"Hmm. Just give me a few more chapters. I'm almost finished." Marylou lowered her eyes to continue reading as she settled herself more comfortably in the bed.

Lifting the remote control level with the television, Bob pressed the button to turn it on. He pressed another and began flipping through the channels until he found one airing a golf game.

Pulling himself up a bit closer against the headboard he reached a hand behind his back to straighten the pillow.

"Lower the sound a little, Honey. would you please?" Marylou asked politely from her side of the bed.

"Sure, Dear." Bob pressed another button and lowered the volume, and then he and his wife settled into a familiar evening of relaxation.

After nearly an hour passed, Marylou closed the back cover to the book she was reading and dabbed the wadded tissue balled in her hand at her eyes and cheeks.

A heavy sigh escaped her lips along with the tiniest whimper.

"You okay, Dear?" Bob asked his wife.

"Oh," her voice quivered. "That was such a sad, sad story."

His brow furrowed as he scratched the side of his head, "Hmm. Good book, huh?"

"Oh yes, it was such a good story. Such a sad, sad story."

Inhaling a long breath, Bob released it slowly and turned his attention back to the golf game on television.

"Good game?" His wife asked.

"Uh huh."

"You can turn it up a little now, if you like."

Bob pressed the volume to move louder and slouched a bit against the pillow.

Her eyes focusing on the television broadcast, Marylou endeavored to concentrate on the golf game too.

She watched one man sidle up to a little white ball, then hit it hard. She heard the whack and as the camera panned out to display the sand pit the ball had fallen in, she rolled her eyes.

"Who's winning?" she asked.

Bob's attention was focused solely on the game and he grunted some kind of response that Marylou did not understand. She nudged him gently on the shoulder.

Startled a bit, he turned to her. "Yeah?'

"You wanna?" His wife raised her eyebrows and grinned.

"The game...it should be over in a few minutes."

For a few minutes, Marylou studied the game on television, then she kissed Bob on the cheek and turned to settle herself for a good night's sleep.

Within ten minutes, Bob yawned as he listened to the broadcasters tout the strategy of the winning player. He yawned again and pressed the button to turn the TV off.

Scrunching his pillow to a desired fullness his eyes rested on his sleeping wife.

A light snore scaped her slightly parted lips. He leaned in to kiss the side of her head before turning the lamp off and pulling the covers over himself.

The following evening, the usual hour, around ten o'clock, Bob and Marylou sat in bed.

She had already begun a new book and he was flipping through the channels.

Suddenly and without warning, he pressed the off button on the remote and jerked the book from his wife's hands.

"You used to call me Bobby."

Gently she wrapped her fingers around the book and pulled it from him. "That was thirty years ago...and speaking of used-to's, you used to tell me how pretty I was."

The couple stared into one another's eyes.

"I love you," Bob said.

"I love you too," Marylou responded. "And we're getting older.

"We're not dead." Bob rolled his eyes. "Maybe we should get some of that enhancement stuff."

As he spoke the words, his wife studied his face sympathetically. "Maybe I should get on some kind of hormone therapy...but to tell the truth, honey, I'm just not that interested anymore."

She could tell her last words had hurt his feelings. His lips turned downward and a bit of color seemed to leave his cheeks.

"But it's not you, dear." She caressed his shoulder with her hand. "It's me...I'm in that menopause thing, I'm sure you've heard of that."

Nodding, Bob lifted his head, "yeah, and things don't work for me like they used to either."

"We're just getting older."

The conversation ended. They gave each other a peck on the lips and rolled on their sides to go to sleep.

φφφφφφφφφ

Marylou walked through the glass door of her office building and nodded to the man holding it open.

"Good morning Marylou, that sweater really brings out your blue eyes."

Cory always greeted her in the mornings at the door—and he always had something nice to say. But Marylou never thought anything of it. She simply thought of him as a polite, nice young man.

131

Marylou considered that the difference in age was probably close to fifteen–maybe a few more–years.

Turning her head a bit to acknowledge his greeting, she found herself swimming in his hazel eyes.

She felt her throat tighten and was suddenly very self-conscious.

"Are you all right?" Cory reached his arm around her shoulder.

"Yes, yes," she said, not wanting to look into his eyes again. "Thank you." She moved from beneath his arm and walked quickly toward her desk.

En route, she passed by the ladies' restroom and quickly turned back to slip through the door.

She looked around past the stalls and multiple sinks–no one else was there. She bent down and looked for feet beneath the stalls. She shook her head, "doesn't seem to be…"

Releasing a breath she brought her hands to her waist and smoothed her blouse, looked in the mirror and examined herself.

I don't look so bad, she thought. "Wish my rear end wasn't so big, but isn't that how they like it these days–a little junk in the trunk?"

She turned sideways and examined her profile. "Good googamooga, they hang down to my elbows." Sliding her fingers beneath her blouse she pulled upwards on the straps to her bra. She nodded, "better."

Letting the straps go, she watched her profile change. She pulled the straps upwards again, then let them go again. "Before," she pulled them up, "after." Pulling and then releasing, Marylou giggled, "before-after, before-after, before-after."

"Okay, whatever it takes to amuse ourselves these days." A familiar voice chuckled.

Shocked by the laughter, Marylou blushed and quickly smoothed her blouse again. "Where did you come from Alice? I didn't see..."

"I got up this morning at five and did a three mile run–still have on my sneakers." She glanced quickly at her feet, "Got to keep myself looking young." The somewhat older woman eyed Marylou's body quickly then glanced away. "Thinking of getting a boob job?" Alice snickered.

"No." Shooting a defiant glance toward her friend and boss, Marylou continued. "It's just that ever since menopause, everything has gone south... or completely disappeared."

"I know the feeling." The older woman sneered. "That's why they make Botox...and other little things for us mature women."

133

Endeavoring to have her examination of Marylou's body look less obvious, she continued, "You need to consider some of those things. The Botox doesn't hurt as badly as you may think and it works wonders."

"Plum Duff," Marylou quipped.

"What?"

"Plum Duff." Marylou repeated.

"What is Plum Duff?" asked Alice.

"It's an old, and I mean old, dessert." Marylou replied. Checking the time on her cell phone, she chuckled, "Better get to work—I'll talk to you later."

Following quickly behind Marylou, Alice glanced quickly in the mirror, cupped her hands under her breasts and winked. "If it's old, it can't be that good."

"Really." Marylou's sardonic retort fell on deaf ears as the two women passed by Cory's desk.

The man looked up and slowly slid his eyes to meet Marylou's.

She felt a tingle where she hadn't felt one in years.

Catching her breath she reprimanded herself. *I'm a happily...* she stopped, the incomplete thought faded from her mind as she sat down at her desk; Cory had turned to watch her. She forced herself to meet his gaze...she smiled shyly before turning her attention to the day's work load.

Has he been doing this all along? she thought as she opened a folder and placed it next to the computer. *For months he has been opening the door for me—could he be interested?*

She lifted her head again. Cory had turned his back and was busy at his station.

φφφφφφφφφ

Grabbing hold of the ladder, Bob treaded water as he pulled the regulator from his mouth.

He lifted the face mask to the top of his head and settled a scraper and large head brush on the dock. Then he removed the mask from his head and pulled himself up the narrow rungs of the ladder, and laid the air tank next to the mask, BCD vest and cleaning instruments.

Standing on the finger dock he studied the layout of Island Marina, and the numerous finger docks that led to the many power boats and sailing vessels docked there.

"Millions of dollars," he spoke aloud. *A boat is a hole in the water you pour money into.*

Sometimes he felt a bit envious of the boat owners with their fancy upscale yachts. But in all the years he'd been working at this marina and others, he'd seldom seen an owner take their boat out for more than a few days a year.

None cleaned their own boats, and most knew next to nothing about the ocean. And wasn't that what it was all about? Wasn't a boat for spending time on the ocean?

Reaching to the back of his neoprene diving suit, Bob unzipped it to his waist, and felt the flop of the paunch he'd been developing over the last several years. It was still there. He patted it, *old friend*, he thought.

Is this why she doesn't want me anymore? Is this why I'm not so enthusiastic?

Bob grabbed his belly and shook it back and forth.

A tap on the port light of the Jarrett Bay he'd just been working on startled him; his face reddened as the owner, Kent Fochet drew a wide grin across his face and called out through the glass, "I've got one of those too."

The muffled words embarrassed Bob, but he smiled back to the man and nodded.

"You know," Kent shouted the words as he climbed the few steps from the galley way to the deck of his forty-six foot yacht, "I was just about your age when I left my first wife."

I know your life story, Kent. I've known you for thirty years. As soon as the thought entered Bob's mind he wondered if the annoyed look showed on his face. He smiled, "Oh, really?"

"Yeah, I was starting to get a little soft in places." Kent patted his stomach; a sly grin crossed his lips as he raised an eyebrow, "around my gut and points south–if you know what I mean."

"Umm," Bob nodded and feigned a mild interest.

"But I got a little lipo and fixed that problem. And the other, well–let's just say–blue is my favorite color."

Bob's interest piqued a bit as he listened to the older man. He pulled his scuba tank closer to the stack of cleaning paraphernalia and walked back toward the stern of the boat where Kent stood; Bob noticed how fit he was–he didn't see any paunch.

I know damn well he's in his sixties. I've got more of a belly than he does.

"Yep, I was about your age–working my ass off–mortgage nearly paid off–kids off to college–

and I started wondering what it was all about. What in the world had I accomplished? Why wasn't I dancing around like the happiest man on earth?" Kent motioned for Bob to come aboard the the Jarrett Bay, one of the finest power yachts available.

"That's when I went out and bought my first real boat. Not some little skiff or fishing boat, but I'm talking about a real boat." He reached a hand to the side of the vessel and patted its fiberglass hull gently.

Settling himself in one of the deck chairs, Kent leaned back, closed his eyes to the warmth of the sun and grinned. "That seems like a lifetime ago."

"This is one the finest pieces of ocean craft, Kent." Bob gazed about, then nodded as he slid into one of the chairs. "Not many people can afford a craft like this."

"Beats the hell out of the trawler." He paused for a moment. "Sorry, sometimes I feel a little guilty about selling that piece of crap to you."

"Don't be sorry. I love that old boat. Me and Marylou are fixing–"

Thrusting his arm forward, Kent interrupted Bob's sentence, "Whatcha think of this?" He touched his fingers to the new cell phone on his wrist and snickered. "Cost a bundle, but isn't it something. I feel like I'm William Shatner on Star Trek."

φφφφφφφφ

"What was that you were talking about when we were leaving the restroom this morning?" Alice leaned forward as she rested her elbows on the table.

"Let's order first. We've only got an hour and I don't want to get fired." Marylou giggled.

Alice's lips drew into a sarcastic smirk, "Okay, okay, don't rub it in. I'm not such a bad boss. And you're with me—I'll write you in if we're late." She leaned back in the dining chair, "It's not such a chore working for me, is it? I haven't changed that much since I took over the business from Kent."

"No," Marylou teased. "I like working for you."

Alice turned her head; spotting the waitress, she raised her hand and snapped her fingers. The waitress appeared instantaneously and smiled, "Yes, Ma'am."

"I'll have the water-cress sandwich with a diet Coke." She handed the menu to the waitress and turned to Marylou.

"I'll have the Reuben with Swiss on rye and a sweet iced tea."

"I think I like going to lunch with you just so I can smell the yummy stuff you get to order. Wish I didn't have to worry about my weight."

Marylou flashed a look of annoyance toward her friend.

"Oh, you know what I mean—you've got such a cute figure—it's just that you don't care if—oh, I mean you're not fat by any means but—"

"I know what you mean Alice. I've never been thin and tall like you—I never will be. It's all plum duff to me."

"There you go again. You said that this morning in the bathroom. Just what are you talking about—plum duff?"

"It's a dessert, an old English dessert—pudding sort of. I think the name has something to do with some kind of sailor's folklore. Anyway, plum duff has no plums."

"It has no plums—then why is it called plum duff? I don't get it."

"Well, it's still sweet and..." Lifting her head, Marylou nodded, acknowledging the waitress as she brought the order and placed it on the table.

"And?" Scrunching her face, Alice glared an annoyed look at her friend.

"And it may not have any plums, but it's still sweet." Marylou studied the food before her, "Looks good."

"Smells good too." Alice placed the napkin in her lap, eyed the salad before her and shrugged.

Holding the sandwich between her fingers, Marylou opened her mouth wide and bit into it; juices splattered down onto the plate below.

Alice could smell the aroma of the freshly cooked meat. She even thought she could feel the warmth of the heated sandwich radiate from across the table. She watched Marylou as she dabbed the corners of her mouth with a napkin and again as her eyes closed when Marylou bit into the Reuben once again.

Sighing, Alice speared a piece of lettuce with her fork.

φφφφφφφφ

"How was work today, dear?" Leaning in to kiss her husband's cheek, Marylou felt his hand go around her waist and pull her close.

141

"I love you." Bob puckered his mouth for another quick peck on his wife's lips. "Worked on Kent Fochet's boat. What a pile of barnacles. He's only had it for a year and I don't think he's taken her out more than two or three times."

Marylou shook her head, "Too bad. I know if we had a boat like that we'd be sailing around the world."

Pulling his shirt over his head, Bob called to his wife as he headed toward the bathroom. "Anything new going on at the office? Your boss lady say anything about giving you those extra two weeks off?"

As she shook her head no, Marylou called out, "She'll come around. She knows I've earned it this year."

Listening as the shower beat a steady rhythm to her husband's out of tune singing, Marylou's thoughts wandered back to the conversation she had been having with Alice Fochet.

She recalled the first time she had met her and Kent at the marina. They were young, their children were all under the age of ten. Kent could barely afford to pay Bob for scraping the hull of his Grady White. a much smaller boat than the one he had now. And smaller too, than the ones the couple had bought in subsequent years.

That was all so long ago.

φφφφφφφφφ

"Good morning!" Cory smiled broadly and held the door open for Marylou, she smiled back at him.

"Hope you had an eventful weekend."

"Naw, not too eventful. My husband Bob and I took the skiff over to Lea Island and did a little fishing and had a picnic. That's all."

"Did you wear your bikini? I bet you look hot in a bathing suit." He searched her face and leaned closer, "You two didn't do any skinny dipping or anything?" His eyes slowly scanned her body. "I hear that's a pretty desolate place this time of year."

Marylou blushed and quickly glanced away from his provocative gaze.

Yes, she was certain of it now. Cory was flirting with her. Nodding politely, she moved past him.

For a moment she felt the warm sensation of acceptance and sexuality. *He finds me attractive,* she thought as she slipped into her office chair. The corners of her lips rising, she looked up and saw him standing with his back to her, as he flipped through the pages of a manual. As he turned the pages, she studied his biceps; even turning a page made them move.

He was lean, but not too lean. His lips were full and his hair thick and wavy. She studied how the arch of his back curved into the rise of his buttocks.

Suddenly he was looking at her. His eyes blazed as the grin on his lips turned into a somewhat crooked smile. It was disarming.

Immediately Marylou lowered her eyes and began typing.

Throughout the day Marylou toyed with the idea of flirting back with Cory. She built scenarios in her mind about the two of them being alone—kissing—touching.

Echoes of youthful vigor and sensuality tickled her thoughts-as she sat in front of the computer. She found that time flew by and before she knew it, it was nearly lunch time.

Usually she and Alice walked next door to the Island Deli but Alice had not shown up for work today. *Oh, one of the perks, I guess, of being the boss lady, you get to take off whenever you like.*

At one o'clock she reached into the desk drawer and pulled out her purse. Rising, she turned and there he was, Cory.

"How about you joining me today?" he asked

Yes, the crooked smile was charming.

"Okay," she smiled back.

"So you live at the beach?" Cory asked.

"No, my husband and I live in Sloop Point, but we take the skiff over to the island all the time."

"Must be nice."

"You must live close by. You're always here so early." Marylou speared a cucumber and crouton.

It was kind of fun flirting with a younger man. She'd seen Alice do it all the time. In fact, Alice flirted with all the men in the office. She'd heard that there had even been an affair or two—and heard about how the men were sleeping their way to the top.

Unconsciously she shook her head as she bit down on the food, immediately she heard the crouton. It sounded so loud and she considered that Cory must have heard her loud munching. She felt foolish.

"Yeah, I live a couple of miles down the road. I try to get here a few minutes early. You know, the early bird gets the worm." Piercing a slice of chicken, Cory cut it with his knife. "Oh," he chuckled gently as he studied Marylou's face. "I think you have some salad dressing on your chin, sweetie." He leaned closer and rubbed a finger across the skin above her upper lip.

"I'm so embarrassed...sorry...I..."

"It's no big deal, sweetie" His finger rubbed against her skin again. "No, it's not dressing."

The puzzled look coupled with distaste filled the younger man's eyes. It prompted Marylou to pull back. She watched Cory pull back too and lower his head. He set his fork down and rose.

"I have to go to the restroom. Be back in a few." Turning, Cory rushed away.

Marylou rubbed the place above her lip. No, there was no dressing or other food bit there. Her finger rubbed more delicately around the area.

Ah, there it is. A HAIR! Quickly she plucked it out and held it before her eyes. *A gray one! A long gray one. Oh my gosh—a gray hair on my upper lip!* She rubbed again and felt even more—though shorter and thinner—more hair. Bob always called it her "peach fuzz." She had never thought anything of it.

The chair felt too small. Her feet could not find a comfortable way or place to be. The fork felt awkward in her hand. She looked up from the salad that now looked so disgusting and there stood Cory. He would not, could not meet her eyes.

φφφφφφφφ

Bob pulled the face mask over his eyes and nose and pushed the regulator into his mouth before jumping into the water.

He had set the brush and scraper in a bag hanging from the side of the boat. Today he was working on a thirty six foot Alubat sloop.

This hull would not be very dirty since the owner actually used his boat for something more than a party vehicle.

The owner, along with his family, had just been in for a few days from Fiji and needed the hull checked and the propeller replaced. It would be an easy job; idle boats were the only ones that ever amassed any barnacles and other trash on their hulls.

Bob imagined that the owners of this boat lived very exciting lives. *Must be nice*, he thought as he swam next to the hull and pulled the brush out of the bag.

He was right—hardly any algae at all.

He loved his job and had been doing it for years. The money was good. It afforded him time to go fishing when he wanted and to spend time with his family. It had even paid for tech school for his son Jack who was now a diesel mechanic at a big marina in Florida.

His daughter Claudia was serving in the Navy in Japan right now.

Continuing to brush along the hull he nodded, the satisfaction he felt about his children, their lives—he was proud that Marylou and he had stuck through the hard and lean times to raise them.

He was still getting used to it being just him and Marylou. Things did feel different, but life felt comfortable.

But then, there were people like Kent and Alice, who after their children left home, didn't stay together. And he wondered sometimes if he was missing out on something. The thought had crossed his mind—*are we still in love*? He knew he loved Marylou. She was his rock and he knew he was hers. Wasn't he?

But in love? Wasn't that what Kent had cited as the reason for his divorce from Alice so many years ago? 'We're just not in love anymore.'

Bob pulled himself up to the dock and settled his arms across the wooden planks, pulled the regulator from his mouth, the face mask from his face, and reached down to slip the flippers from his feet.

Gazing toward Kent Fochet's watercraft he listened to the loud music coming from the stern. He pulled his body upward to sit on the dock. For a few seconds he watched the young woman as she swayed about to the tunes. Her skimpy bikini barely covered her breasts.

As she moved, her hips and thighs moved to the beat of the music.

Mesmerized, Bob did not hear Kent call to him.

"Hey! Bob-o-lou...hey! Bobbo...hey! Bobbette." Fochet called again and again. Finally he turned the music down and repeated the callings. "Hey! Bob-o-lou!"

Jerking his head to the man's voice, Bob waved.

"Come on over and join us." Kent shouted.

"Yeah, come join us." The tall, buxom woman with long red hair bounced about as she waved.

Bob stacked his tank and flippers, mask and other diving paraphernalia in a heap next to Kent's boat and climbed aboard.

"Bob, I'd like you to meet my new wife-to-be, Deirdre. Isn't she a beauty?"

Nodding, Bob smiled, doing his best to avoid looking at any part of her sparsely clothed body other than her eyes.

"Take that big condom off and join us," Kent laughed raucously. "You do have something on under that don't you?"

"Under my wetsuit?" Bob asked sheepishly.

"Bet he's got a Speedo on." Another woman's voice cooed as she emerged from below deck.

"Well, maybe I should just keep it on."

"You do! You do have a Speedo on underneath your wetsuit!" the woman, much shorter than Deirdre, giggled. Her short brown hair curled about her freckled face as she laughed.

"Oh, Bob—this is Kismet," Kent said.

A puzzled look crossed his face. He mouthed the word kismet and cocked his head to the side.

Kent threw his head back and laughed loudly again.

"Kismet, Deirdre's cousin visiting from Iowa. Kismet is this fine young woman's name, Bob. This is the first time she's ever seen the ocean. Now what do you think of that?" He winked. "She lives on a farm up there in Iowa."

"I'm about as country as you can get, Bobby."

It had been years since anyone had called him Bobby. And even longer since any woman had looked at him the way Kismet was doing just now.

"Nobody cares what you have on under your wetsuit; just have a beer with us." Kent held out a bottle of St. Pauly Girl and motioned toward the cooler on the deck. "Help yourself."

Bob leaned to open the cooler. He grabbed a bottle of Budweiser and took a sip.

Unzipping his suit to the waist, he struggled to pull his arms out.

"Here, let me help you with that, Kismet giggled.

Instantly Bob thrust the beer forward for the woman to hold as he pulled his arms free and tied the lose neoprene arms behind his back.

A bit self-conscious about his paunch, he rested an arm across it as he relaxed against the gunwale.

"So you clean the bottoms of boats—that's what Kent says. Don't you get tired of doing the same thing over and over again?" Kismet asked teasingly.

Bob shrugged, "It's not so bad. Every boat's different." He paused and then added, "Don't you get bored shucking corn all year long?"

"I do other things." The woman winked and rolled a shoulder.

Taking a long swig from the beer, Bob considered the suggestive answer and tone in which it was delivered. He cast a quick look over to Kent who arched an eyebrow and grinned.

"Like, horseback riding and hunting. That's what I meant." Kismet slid a knowing glance toward Kent and then Bob. "You naughty boys. What did you think I meant?"

"My wife, Marylou and I used to go horseback riding."

Kismet eyed Bob's left hand, "You're married? Where's your ring? I always heard that when a married man doesn't wear a ring, he really doesn't want to be married."

"I don't wear my ring when I work."

"Honey, Kismet, sweetie—little fish with sharp teeth like shiny things and so it's not wise to wear jewelry when you dive." Kent interjected and winked.

Bob nodded, "That's right," he added the words too quickly as he shifted his body toward Kent's. "So, when's the big day, my friend—when are you and Deirdre getting married?"

"February fourteenth, Valentine's Day." Drawing his arm around Deirdre, Kent pulled the woman into his lap. "Number three's the lucky charm."

Deirdre's long hair covered the couple's faces as they engaged in a lengthy kiss.

Feeling uncomfortable with the displays of affection, Bob rose and turned toward the dock where his scuba gear lay piled in a neat heap.

"Have another," Kismet handed Bob a beer from the cooler. Glancing toward the couple the young woman smirked, "They're a little nauseating, don't you think?" Crinkling her nose, she added a delicate giggle.

He turned the bottle up and chugged half-way through the brew. "I need to get my gear in the truck." Guzzling the remaining beer, Bob stepped from the boat.

"I'll help."

Bob wasn't sure if he wanted to hear those words or not. But he did nothing to stop Kismet as she too stepped from the boat and walked beside him.

Together they carried the gear to Bob's truck and placed it in the topper covered bed.

"Thanks," Bob turned to the woman.

Tiptoeing to reach her arms around his neck, she kissed his cheek. "You're a nice man. Your wife is a lucky woman."

As he thought of Marylou, he pictured her smile. "Yes, I know."

"I've got a husband back in Iowa. He didn't want to come down here with me. So I just came with Deirdre." She nodded and took another sip of her beer. "He..." Kismet's voice quivered.

Oh no, thought Bob, another drama story. *I don't want to get caught up in that.*

"I just don't know what..." the words grew jumbled as Kismet began crying–sobbing.

"No, no–now, don't you cry. Everything is going to be all right." Bob patted the woman's shoulder.

"But, people just don't understand. Billy says all these mean things to me and I don't know if I–" The blubbering increased as her sobbing grew louder. Kismet leaned into Bob.

"Okay, you two. You better behave yourselves," called Kent as he and Deirdre walked arm in arm along the dock. "We're going to drive up to the grocery store."

"Take care of my cousin," called Deirdre with a laugh as they passed by.

"I left my cover-up on the boat. Could we get it?" Kismet cooed as she wiped tears from her cheeks.

I need to get in the truck and get out of this mess, thought Bob.

But he didn't do that. He politely walked the distraught woman to the boat and inside the cabin where her garment was.

Before sitting down she retrieved a couple more beers from the cooler and offered one to Bob.

Sobbing between sips of the beer, Kismet leaned against him. Again she lit into the drama she had been so pitifully recounting before.

He could smell her youth, coupled with the sourness of the Budweiser. How many had it been— four or five? He couldn't remember. Maybe it had been six. But either way, right now, he had to pee.

Trying to push her from him, Bob attempted to rise from the settee where they were sitting, but she whimpered loudly and tugged at the floppy arms of his wet suit. "You need to take that off," she pawed at him; moaning softly, growling.

Is she laughing or crying? he thought as he pulled away. One minute it was one and the next minute it was the other. Now, she was talking about how cute his nose was and how she loved older men.

The urge to urinate grew stronger and stronger as Bob inched away from the woman to search for the small closet-like room that housed a toilet. Finding the door to the head, he pulled it open, it was filled with stanchions and nautical hardware that had never been used or taken out of the wrapping.. *I should have known, Kent doesn't ever take the boat out. He never needs a toilet–pees over the side when and if he does.*

I can't wait any longer. Bob thought–his impatience increasing, he rushed toward the galley way and climbed the stairs. "Kismet, I have to take a whiz, be back in a minute."

Stepping from the boat to the dock, Bob made his way to the marina restrooms. Reaching for the door, he pulled to open it. "Damn. It's locked."

Glancing at his watch he noticed the time, and exhaled, "Marylou's going to be pissed; I'm usually home two hours ago."

156

Scanning the marina and boats, he searched for a place where he would have the privacy to pee. He walked along a far finger dock and pushed down the bottom part of his wet suit.

The relief was immeasurable. "Ahhh." He sighed aloud.

"Geez amighty!" The words cut through the silent night like an air horn.

Turning too quickly, Bob exposed himself to Kismet.

As fast as he could, he pulled the neoprene up to cover himself. "I'm sorry, Kismet. I didn't know you were there."

"Gosh damn. I had to pee too. You know," she slurred her words. "But that's the baggiest darn butt I've ever seen in my life. I mean, the skin is just hanging under those cheeks." She laughed a drunken laugh. "Back home when somebody's got a butt like that we say they got noassatol. You know, no-ass-at-all. It's a disease, noassatol." She laughed louder and then spewed vomit all over the dock.

"I think I'm drunk again—Billy says I got a drinking problem."

φφφφφφφφφ

"So you want to have three weeks off in November?" Alice leaned back in her office chair. "You want an extra three weeks?"

"Yep, that's what I'd like to have, Alice. I've been working for you for twenty years now and getting only one week off for vacation and this year, Bob and I would like to have a little more time to do what we've been dreaming about."

"And what is that?"

"We want to take that new boat..."

"You mean the old one y'all bought from me and Kent back—oh geez, how many years ago was that?"

"We've been working on it—it's an older boat—wooden." Marylou nodded. "It's been lots of fun, over the years, working on it."

A perplexed scowl covered Alice's face and she shrugged. "Whatever floats your boat."

"Yeah." Nodding, Marylou smiled. "We want to take the boat and cruise on down the Intracoastal as far as we can until it's time to turn around and come back."

"Doesn't sound that exciting to me. And you think three more weeks will do it for you?"

"I figured I better not push my luck–you are, after all, the boss lady. not just my friend. And that has been a sticky place to be. Sometimes work and friendship don't go together so well. But, so far, so good. And I thought I'd give it a shot and ask you.

Bob and I aren't getting any younger and we'd like to do this before–well, while we're still relatively young."

"Young. Just what does young mean?" Alice presented the question rhetorically. "Kent and I were nearly your age when we really started being successful."

"And when you split up." Marylou slid her eyes above her glasses and caught Alice's gaze.

Alice nodded, her eyes swept the walls of her office; she perused the plaques and awards tacked here and there among the various paintings."I noticed the last time I drove by your place ,that the boat was still on chocks.

Nodding, Marylou smiled gently, "Like I said we've been working on it a long time, but I think we've worked out all the chinks and have her as sea worthy as she's going to get–we just have one more little thing to do." She looked at Alice and grinned. "We just want to get away and enjoy each other."

159

Alice nodded, "I guess, you two deserve it. Go ahead, take the extra weeks. In fact, take one more and really enjoy yourselves.

φφφφφφφφ

"I got the paint." Bob called as he walked toward the trawler, its bare transom shined clean in the morning sunlight.

"Then this is it?" Marylou tied the blue bandanna behind her head and inhaled deeply. "I can't believe it. One more thing and we'll be ready to go."

"Nice of Alice to give you a whole month, my love." He kissed her lips and chuckled, "My little peach fuzz." He studied her lips and laughed again, slowly brought his forefinger and thumb together and plucked out a long gray hair.

"That's a stubborn one. Keeps coming back." He laughed and kissed her again.

"You're sure the paint will be dry enough by tomorrow for us to put her in the water?"

Bob nodded and set the can of paint down in front of the transom. "Got the stencils and brushes–this won't take us an hour and by noon it should be dry. We could leave today if we wanted."

"I still have to fill the galley—need do a little grocery shopping before we go." Sliding her arm around her husband's waist, Marylou reached down to cup his buttocks. She squeezed her hand and giggled, "My butt-less wonder, you have done such a good job repairing the boat. I'm so proud of you."

Taping the stencils to the transom Marylou continued, "Hope you got the right color."

Smiling, Bob settled onto one of the chairs set before the transom. He pried open the can of paint and dipped a brush into it, "Yes,dear—red. That was the color we settled on, right?"

Marylou plopped down in the seat next to her husband and dipped another brush into the paint can. "Yep—red is right—that's the color."

"Could be purple."

"Well, never was too fond of purple."

As the couple finished painting the lettering on their boat, they leaned back. Each sighed as they turned to one another.

"I love you," she said.

"I love you too," Bob echoed

"Good name," Marylou laid the paintbrush across the lip of the can and squeezed her husband's hand.

Bob nodded as he leaned into his wife and read the words written on the boat's transom—PLUM DUFF.

TONIGHT
WE ARE YOUNG

What the night brings—or can

The menu was one sheet of laminated paper printed on both sides.

Helen grasped it with her fingers, thanking the waitress, then wiped a smudge away with a napkin.

Focusing her eyes through the no-line bifocal lenses of her glasses, she read the list of foods.

The list was short—mainly burgers, fries, sandwiches and local seafood. The Sea Gull restaurant, situated next to the island fishing pier, despite its fantastic view, was not on the list of must-go places on Topsail Island. Locals were the main clientele.

It wasn't like Helen to come to such a greasy spoon, but she'd heard that the grouper was the best. Unlike most of the other restaurants on the beach, the Sea Gull's seafood was not overcooked nor over breaded.

She set the menu on the table and looked about the room. It was nearly empty, but then it was late October and most of the tourists were gone for the year. Only a few fisherman hung on, endeavoring to catch fresh seafood of their own.

Maybe I'll just go to Thomas Seafood and buy some fish and cook it myself. That way I know it'll be right.

Feeling a sigh escape her lips, Helen let the numbness of defeat wash over her as she spread her fingers on the table.

She studied them, lifting the left forefinger to examine the mottled red and gray area where she'd burned herself a few weeks before.

Helen knew this scar would never completely fade away; they never do on old skin.

Sliding her eyes to gaze out of the big plate glass window, she puckered her lips, gathering the wrinkled flesh about her mouth. Unlike her, the ocean had definitely not aged. It looked beautiful and beckoning as always, even in the twilight.

No, if I want fried fish, I better let someone else cook it for me.

Inspecting her aging hands again, Helen rubbed the arthritic nodules on her fingers; there was no hiding the bumps and twisting of her once smooth and beautiful hands.

She wore turtle neck sweaters or high collared blouses to hide her twaddle, the creeping of her neck and decolletage, and pants to hide her vein-ridden legs.

Long ago she'd given up wearing short sleeves, now they were at least three-quarter length.

Oh yes, she knew she was vain—always had been. Always had liked things being just so—her body being just so. Not perfect, mind you. But trim, neat, pretty.

But there was no way to hide her hands. She'd considered gloves—maybe in the 1950s or 60s that would have worked, but not now. Gloves were passé.

Rocking her shoulders back and forth, holding back a laugh, she reflected on the notion that time had played a cruel joke on her. Despite all efforts she was forced to accept that youth was gone. Her hands had held on to it for as long as they could. Now, in her mid-seventies she had relinquished all dreams, all could-have-beens.

The fact is, I'm old now. What is it that they say? she asked herself. *'Getting old isn't for sissies.'*

She tapped the table, and tittered lightly, *Things could be worse—look at poor old Edna, she can't remember who she is.*

"Yes ma'am. Are you ready to order?" The voice of the pudgy young waitress startled her. She watched as the girl licked her lips and rested a pencil against an ordering pad.

Helen grinned and perused the girl's youthful body. *I used to have skin like that–maybe not as much of it, but youth is youth.* She smiled as she lifted her face to respond to the waitress.

"I'd like a glass of iced tea, the garden salad and the fried grouper." She stared at the girl's name tag, reading the name 'Lind-z'.

Ah, youth. Helen smiled again at the young girl. "Now, please be sure to tell the chef not to overcook my fish."

"What sides?" The girl nodded. "Carlos never overcooks anything." She added, haughtily this time, "What sides?"

"How about some French fries and cole slaw– and I do get hush puppies with that?"

"Yep." The girl turned and walked briskly through the kitchen door; it swung widely open and shut for several seconds.

Glancing at her hands again, Helen set them in her lap, took a breath and scanned the room of the small restaurant.

From her booth she counted seven more booths and six tables.

There were pictures on the knotty pine walls of days past when the building had been called The Beach Grill. Then, she was a regular–sort of. Her parents accompanied her to the grill every week or so. She was never allowed to come alone.

She saw herself enter through the screen door of the old restaurant–back then–when there were only a few tables, mostly stools stood along a wooden counter. A jukebox was always playing popular tunes. Young boys and girls in swim suits laughed and joked–played tunes and danced.

There had been so much laughter–and slamming of the screen door as youthful boys and girls ran from the restaurant to the beach and back.

Helen recalled longing to be one of them.

I always liked getting a strawberry shake. I remember asking the boy behind the counter for French fries and a strawberry shake.

Once again Lind-z startled Helen as she slid a damp glass of cold tea in front of her, then a wax paper bag of silverware.

The girl didn't add any comment or even look at Helen; she simply set the items on the table and turned to leave.

"Could I have my salad first?" Helen called after her.

The girl turned abruptly, "I'll see if it's ready."

I could complain about the service, Helen considered as she eyed the silverware and tea. *The girl is not very hospitable.*

"It wouldn't do any good," A voice interrupted her thoughts as if they had been read.

Helen lifted her head to meet a familiar face, though one she had never gotten to know very well.

"They're all like that. It's the youth these days— all about themselves. Not many are polite—but you take my grandson, Ben. He's a good one. My daughter taught him right and he's always thoughtful—proud of that young man."

Looking up into the face of the man, Helen nodded and generated a smile—a shy smile. This man had always made her smile.

"Come on now, you know me, Helen. We've known each other forever." His eyes gently begged.

"Buddy. I know you, Buddy. I've known you forever." Her grin turned into a broad smile. "You went to Dixon High."

"You were at Topsail...rivals."

"But *we* never were. Were we?" she added.

The lightness of Buddy's eyes receded as he rested against the table. He was still tall, though not quite as in his youth. His once thick brown hair had thinned a bit. She noticed the brown and pink scars about his brow and nose. *Must have had a bit of skin cancer,* she thought. *He was always outside, doing something.*

For a second, the young Buddy, the one with the broad shoulders and muscular legs, flashed in her mind as one of the teenagers who used to frequent The Beach Grill; she smiled again.

"Oh, I'm sorry. Please sit down. Join me for dinner. Have you had dinner?" Helen asked.

Turning toward the waitress at the counter, Buddy called, "the grilled shrimp, green beans, applesauce...tea," then settled his still powerful frame in the seat opposite Helen.

His hands spread wide before him, he nodded. "Been a long time, huh?"

"I saw you last at Annie's funeral. Wasn't it?"

"My wife."

Helen nodded. "I'm sorry for you, Buddy." Reaching out she touched his fingers. "That's been a couple of years ago. You were with a young woman then." Helen paused.

"My daughter, Tessa. She and my grandson come over every now and then. She's done a good job with him. Ben, I'm proud of him, he's thoughtful–" Pausing for a moment, Buddy nodded and chuckled, "Oh, I guess I already told you that."

"I do it too, repeat myself sometimes." She met his eyes.

"I know you must be lonely now. Are you still by yourself?" Her eyes widened.

Buddy leaned back in the booth, settling his hands on either side of his body. "Now, you know I'm never without a woman for very long–isn't that what you're expecting me to say, Helen?"

Sliding her eyes toward the big glass window, Helen felt her face warm. "I guess you could say that."

She turned to face him, "You always were a rounder–a lady's man."

"Oh, you just thought I was."

"Always a girl on your arm. Always a different girl on your arm."

"Could have been you, Helen," he teased and winked.

As she folded her hands in front of her on the table, Helen reflected on precise words she and Buddy had spoken decades ago. They had been few, but they had been final words spoken between two willful people.

'Why?' he had asked, and she had responded, 'You're not my type.'

"You never gave me a chance." Buddy moved his hands to cover Helen's. "And you were such a pretty girl. Smart too." He cocked his head to the side. "You weren't very outgoing, were you?"

For a moment she shifted her eyes away from his. *I didn't know what to say or how to act when I was young.*

"You were very popular, all the girls..." Helen started.

"Yeah," Buddy half laughed, "I always liked you though."

"Oh?" Exhaling lightly, Helen raised an eyebrow and pulled her hand from beneath his. "That was so long ago."

"Well, here you go." Lind-z settled a platter before Helen along with a bowl of chopped lettuce and tomatoes.

Considering whether or not to mention to the waitress that she had asked for the salad to come first, Helen caught Buddy's gaze. He shrugged and chuckled.

"Oh, what's the use?" Helen tittered.

"And here's your fried shrimp," Lind-z slid another platter before Buddy.

"I thought you ordered grilled," Helen searched for the waitress to respond.

"Oh, that's alright. Can't have everything you want in life." Buddy shrugged. He looked to the waitress and nodded.

As the two elderly people began eating their meals, each wandered back in time to their youth.

Helen recalled Buddy very well. He had been so handsome and outgoing. He always had something funny to say and made everybody laugh, even her, and even when she didn't want to.

Buddy had been on the basketball team. And every couple of weeks, his school played against hers.

Her father, an avid basketball fan, drove to every game. Helen loved going to the games, it was one of the only times she got to participate in any social activities.

She remembered searching for Buddy—watching as he dribbled the ball up the court to make a basket. She recalled how the crowd cheered and clapped for him. And the girls, the cheerleaders...

Helen remembered too, the ambivalent feelings she had for Buddy back then. She wanted to like him. She was very attracted to him and could feel her insides flutter when he looked at her.

But the girls, the cheerleaders, prom queens, they were all over him. It seemed every week there was a new one on his arm.

How many times had she caught him kissing a girl behind the bleachers? And then, there was that time when she was walking through the parking lot to retrieve a forgotten sweater. Passing by his dark green Packard, she noticed how the windows were fogged and how the car rocked to and fro.

Helen would never allow herself to be just another girl to be kissed one night and left the next.

The fish was not overcooked. It was perfect. Helen savored the fresh flavor as she thought of days long gone. Her eyes rose to examine Buddy, he grinned back at her and popped another shrimp in his mouth.

She was pretty. Always quiet though. But she was always nice to me, always polite. But she seemed so serious all the time.

Would she have held me back? I thought so back then. 'We have different interests.' 'You're a nice boy, Buddy, but you're just not my type.' That's what she told me the one time I asked her out. She wouldn't even give me a chance.

I don't think she ever went steady with anyone. Never saw her with any boys.

Buddy shrugged and looked at Helen, even now in her seventies, she was pretty–composed as always.

With her napkin in her lap and the way she sipped her tea and cut her fish–she was gentle, she was proper.

Who was that she married? Some fella from Raleigh? I heard they had a couple of kids.

Lowering his eyes as he scooped a spoonful of applesauce into his mouth, Buddy thought of Annie–it had been two years since her passing. Of his three wives, he had been with her the longest.

Soon after high school he'd met his first wife. She was a lot of fun. They'd had a lot of fun together. Charlotte –"Char"–, she enjoyed going out on the boat and fishing, skiing, scuba diving, and all the partying,

She also liked Mike, his business partner, his ex-business partner. *How long had they been married now?*

Wasn't that about the time I saw Helen at a football game? Duke was playing Carolina.

180

He caught a glimpse of Helen in his mind's eye. She'd let her hair grow long and straight back then. She wore those round rim glasses...she was still pretty.

I know she saw me—looked right at me. Didn't she smile?

No, I remember. She was sitting with some man in a light blue blazer—some frat boy—and yes, she did smile at me. I lost sight of her though.

He contemplated the scene—*I was with that girl—the one I was dating after the divorce, the one with the enormous boobs—she was with me.*

Raising his head, Buddy glanced at Helen as she carefully cut the grouper with a fork. *Maybe if I had had a girl like Helen.*

"So, what have you been doing all these years, Buddy? I know you were always adventurous. I bet you've led a very interesting life."

He shrugged. "The business was good to me. Never got filthy rich, but I've done okay."

She nodded, "The boat business?"

"Yes, started that right out of high school."

Helen nodded again as she took a sip of tea.

"Done a little bit of traveling too—mostly through the business, of course."

Helen drew back her shoulders, her eyes brightened with interest. "Oh. How exciting. Where did you go?"

"Spent some time in the islands, the Caribbean."

She nodded. "Um, lots of white sand beaches." Helen pictured Buddy lolling about on a beach with scantily clad women, sipping mixed drinks.

"And then I went down to South America a few times, Europe…Germany, France, Netherlands… Russia."

Her disparaging expression turned into one of wonder, "Did you sell boats there?"

"No. Not really. They were just places I was led to, so to speak. My second wife loved to travel."

"Oh."

"But I really enjoyed it. Learned a lot about the world by visiting those places."

Her eyes met his, despite the turned up lips, his eyes belied weariness.

"Really? All of those places, how interesting. I always wanted to travel but Tom was never interested in the rest of the world."

"Tom, that was your husband's name." Buddy settled his fork and napkin on the top of his plate.

"I never did meet him, but I heard that you two married while in college."

His eyes squinting, Buddy pursed his lips and rubbed his chin, "I think I saw him once, when we were young, at a football game in Raleigh.

"That would have been him," Helen said aloud, thinking that it would have had to have been Tom, since he was the only man she had ever dated.

"Hmm," Looking pensively into her faded green eyes he spoke, "I hope you have had a good life."

Dabbing the corners of her lips with the paper napkin, Helen settled it to the side of her plate. "I have. My children are successful, one lives close by. I finally got a cook book I've been working on for years, published." Gently nodding, the corners of her lips turned upward. "Yes, I think I've had a good life."

Buddy reached for her hand and held it gently in his own. "I'm glad." Thrusting his head forward a bit, he winked.

Helen sighed gently, "We can't have control over everything in our lives."

He released her hand and nodded, "That's for sure." Grinning broadly he chuckled, "Never thought I'd be married three times."

"But you were happy, weren't you? With this last one—Annie?"

Buddy's eyes shifted to gaze out the window; he settled his feet beneath the table to a more comfortable position. "Hmm, I was with her the longest—eighteen years..." He rubbed a finger over his wrinkled lips and paused. "What about you? Were you happy?"

As she pushed the half empty glass of tea away from her plate, the corners of her lips drew into a line. "I was with him my whole life."

Clearing his throat, Buddy reached for his glass of tea and drank heartily. He shook his head. "I'd say I had a good life, I've done lots of things, been lots of places, been around the block a few times, made lots of friends. Made even more money and lost a hell of a whole lot of that because of friends and those blocks I went around." He sat silent for a moment, "Nobody gets everything they want. But do I feel empty?" Buddy lifted his shoulders and shifted in his seat, "I do wonder sometimes what life would have been like if I had chosen a different path. If I had lived a different kind of life. I think I may have missed out on some things by not staying with one person. I don't have the best relationship with my children." *Maybe if I had been with a woman like you.* Buddy's eyes lifted to meet Helen's; they held hers.

He had always been so bold, so abrupt. That was one of the things that had scared her away from him. In her youth and even into her mid-life, sudden change, anything out of her routine–these types of things had made her uncomfortable.

But a miscarriage had come suddenly, the loss of her home by fire had come suddenly, Tom's death had come suddenly. There had been other things too, that had happened suddenly and now, sudden was complacent and expected.

I wish I knew then what I know now. The corners of Helen's eyes gathered in folds as she tittered a low "I know what you mean."

Pushing both his and her plates aside, Buddy looked gently into her eyes. "You never know how it's going to turn out, do you?" He grabbed Helen's hands firmly and added, "Oh, what it would have been like for you and me."

"If I hadn't have been so scared, so shy, so..."

"Proper."

Nodding, Helen added, "And you..."

"It was all about having fun."

"But that's what youth is? Isn't it?"

"I was young for a long time—didn't want to grow up."

Helen rose, moved across the table to slide next to Buddy in the booth.

Raising her fingers to his lips, he kissed the tips. He stroked them lightly.

The couple held hands and stared beyond the plate glass window to the movement of the waves, frothing as they licked the shore.

The lights of the fishing pier danced on the illuminated water below; suddenly Helen felt whimsical and light.

"You remember this place back when..."

"I used to come here every weekend—had a blast."

"It was different," Laughing, Helen could feel his warmth.

"Everything was different."

"I wish..."

Buddy pushed against her body. "Let's go for a walk." The excitement in his voice startled her, but she rose immediately and the two made their way out the door and down the steps to the sand, where they both kicked off their shoes.

He leaned against the banister of the stairs and grabbed her hand. Pulling Helen close he studied the softness of her face.

Silently they walked toward the water, it felt cool on their feet as they strolled along the shore.

Lind-z stood at the window of the Sea Gull Restaurant watching as the elderly couple walked away from the lights of the fishing pier.

"Well, there goes my tip." She groaned. "These old farts around here are always forgetting to pay."

She walked out onto the porch of the restaurant and settled her hands on her hips considering whether or not to call out to them.

"Probably won't hear me anyway," she muttered.

Still standing on the porch she watched as the couple, arm in arm, walked farther and farther away.

The tinkle of laughter filled the night air for a brief moment.

Lind-z's brow furrowed as she squinted her eyes to search into the darkness for the two. "Where'd they go?"

"We're almost there." Buddy wrapped his arm around Helen's shoulder and pulled her long hair to the side of her neck. He looked up into the nearly starless night sky.

Helen let go a raucous laugh that shocked Buddy—it was so out of character. But he liked it. The girl was there, the young girl he'd liked when he was a boy—she was gazing back at him, playful, with only a hint of the timidity there once had been. *Could this be?* he asked himself.

Helen closed her eyes, and there he was—the young man. She opened them, and he laughed—just like the laughing, always bold, Buddy.

She dare not think it was only her imagination that his touch felt so young and alive too.

In the darkness, she heard a whisper, "Tonight we are young."

And Helen felt young. Unencumbered by the shackles of age, she leaned into Buddy's warmth, nestling her head against his shoulder.

"Will you go out with me?" he asked.

His cadence was quicker and so was his gait. How was she keeping up with him?

Helen breathed in the salty sea air, closed her eyes and answered, "Oh yes! Yes! I'd love to."